Marked Heart

A Marked Heart Novel

M. Sembera

Marked Heart
Copyright 2015 © M. Sembera
ISBN: 978-0692500156
Edited by Lucii Grubb
Cover Design Copyright 2015
© M. Sembera
g-stockstudio, R-O-M-A/Shutterstock
Published by
Broken Bird Media

For more information contact:
M.Sembera@brokenbirdmedia.com
Marked Heart is a work of fiction. All names, Characters, places and incidents are the product of the author's imagination.

Place name and any resemblance to events or actual persons, living or dead, are entirely coincidental.

Lily vector art featured with quote provided by Naddya/Shutterstock

The Wren and Celtic Heart logo is an original piece of art created specifically for M. Sembera. All Rights reserved by Broken Bird Media.

'We're not good for each other.' ~Liv

'Let's be bad then.' ~Braden

To my Mom, for showing me how to survive, overcome,

and find the strength to persevere with love.

Table of Contents

A marked heart, longing for the one is nothing more than a restless heart, burdened by a lie.

Prologue

The street lights flickered on as Braden came to a stop. Just ahead of him was The Dog House; the bar his family owned, his oldest brother Auggie tended, his sister in law Charlotte managed and the location of his sister Penny's engagement party. There he had his first drink, his heart broken, his ass kicked and his last performance as a musician. Taking a deep breath, he shook his head at himself. So much had changed over the last year. In a family where everyone has their place, he honestly couldn't see where he fit into it anymore.

Braden felt lost in the shuffle of life. All he ever wanted to do was sing and play guitar. He had been in love with the same girl since high school. Time after time he had listened to her lie, took her back after she had cheated and believed her when she said she loved him. But, he finally saw the light the night her husband gave him the beating of his life. He held it together for as long as he could but after his drummer and best friend betrayed him, by cheating on his sister with the very girl who had made a career out of breaking his heart, he didn't have the heart for it anymore.

Even something as simple as listening to the radio became unbearable.

If it weren't for the fact that it was Penny and Seth's party, he wouldn't have shown up at all.

It started to drizzle, causing Braden to glance up and mentally reply, 'Alright, I'm going,' as he made his way to the open doors of the bar. He had only taken two steps when he saw his cousin's wife, Liv, walk out.

His sister Penny's voice echoed out of the doors, "Liv!" before he saw her step out of the bar.

Unaffected by Penny's shout, Liv continued swiftly walking in his direction.

"Braden, stop her!" she exclaimed before ducking back into the bar.

The moment his sister disappeared, Liv was right beside him. Before she could pass him by, he reached his hand out and caught the top of her arm.

Liv stopped. She continued to stare straight ahead, without moving or speaking, she just stood there. Braden let go of her arm, since it was clear she wasn't going anywhere, and stepped in front of her. She didn't have to say a word for him to know she was wounded. Liv blinked twice before glancing up at him. Even though her face held no expression, the look in her eyes made is chest burn and his stomach hurt.

In a split second, they were surrounded by his family. As they crowded around, the drizzle turned into a light mist of rain. Braden noticed Penny crying and Charlotte had tears in her eyes. Seth's expression was anguished as he kept his head down, staring at the ground with his arms around Penny. Looking to Auggie for an explanation, it took his brother several minutes to get the words out.

Wearing the same sorrowful scowl as when they lost their dad and when their brother Will passed, Auggie cleared his throat, informing, "Oran was on his way here and saw Kieran's truck rolled over a mile out from the farmhouse." Braden's heart sank as his brother shook his head and continued, "He took most of the guard rail with him but ya know, it's a pretty steep drop off."

Nodding, Braden glanced back at Liv just as their cousin Jackson walked up.

"They're fairly certain it was instant. The impact..." Jackson paused as his wife, Ren, stepped next to Liv saying, "I'm going to take you to our house." Placing her arm around Liv's shoulders.

There was no response from Liv, not even a flinch as she silently walked away with Ren while Penny and Charlotte followed close behind them.

The second, the girls were out of ear shot, Jackson continued.

"Most of his upper body was crushed on impact. He wasn't wearing a seatbelt."

Seth spoke up, asking, "Do they know what caused it?"

With a heavy sigh, Jackson replied, "They are assuming he was texting and driving. His phone was a few feet from the truck. It showed a partial unsent message from him and then a few from another number asking why he wasn't answering her."

"Her?" Seth questioned before asking, "He was texting Liv when it happened?"

"No." Jackson stated with a hint of disappointment in his eyes.

Instantly furious, Braden glared at Auggie as he questioned, "Is there anything we can do to keep Liv from finding out?"

"Ren could call in a favor, but I would prefer to take another route. They took it to the station as evidence for the police report. Anybody know somebody?"

Staring at all of them in disbelief as Seth replied, "If they let one of us pick it up, we could just erase it." Braden couldn't believe what he was hearing.

"That bastard was cheating on her and y'all are gonna cover his ass so she doesn't find out?"

"I never said that he was cheating." Jackson clarified before saying, "But, from what the officer read me, he was assuring whoever it was that he was going to leave Liv."

"And that's not cheating?"

Auggie quickly turned to him, griping, "Her husband is dead. How hurt do you want her?" Irritation settled inside of Braden as he realized they were right. He disagreed with their decision completely. However, knowing that if she found out it would only cause her more pain, he relented.

~

Six months after his cousin Kieran's funeral, things had somewhat gone back to normal. Braden took a job at Stockman's Superior Warehouse and Supply, after his old friend, Pat Stockman, came back to town to take over his family's business. The job was boring and monotonous but the pay was great and more than enough to get him off of Penny's couch and into his own apartment.

Everyone seemed impressed with how well Liv was taking the loss. She was at Legacy Ink, the tattoo shop that now belonged to her since her husband was dead, all day every day with the exception of Sundays. Since Kieran's death, the shop thrived in his absence. He was happy for them although he could have done without knowing why it was suddenly so popular. Apparently, getting tattooed by a skilled red head, while enjoying the view of the dark haired assistant with criminally tight pants and full sleeve tattoos, was a huge turn on. He guessed he would have seen the draw himself, had it not been for the fact that it was his sister Penny and Liv.

No matter what everyone else thought, he felt differently. Her voice wasn't the same and even though he hadn't seen her since the funeral, somehow he felt like he was carrying her sadness with him. Braden made a habit of calling Liv to check on her every evening on the way home from work. Each time hoping he would hear something that would alleviate the heaviness in his heart.

Blowing in his hands to keep them warm, he knew he should have warmed up his car before getting in. Braden's 1970 Chevrolet El Camino was his baby but on cold nights like tonight she really showed her age. It was April for cryin' out loud, and only forty two degrees. Pulling the hood of his dark gray hoodie over his head as he crossed his arms across his chest, Braden mumbled to himself about how much he hated cold weather.

When warmth finally started to flow from the vents into the cab, he shook off the stiffness from his shivering, pulled his cell phone out of his pocket, and dialed Liv's number.

After seven rings he heard her voicemail, "Speak your peace."

Even though their nightly conversations mostly consisted of 'Hey', 'You need anything', 'Nah', 'Later', it bothered him that she hadn't answered. He tried again.

"Speak your peace."

Why wasn't she answering?

"Speak your peace."

She always answered.

"Speak your peace."

Heated from frustration, Braden flipped the vent away from him and sent her a text.

B: Answer your phone.

L:

B: Hello! Liv!

L:

He made one last attempt to call her.

"Speak your peace."

Hot enough to feel himself starting to sweat, Braden cracked the window, allowing cold air to rush in, before backing out of the parking lot. Switching between feeling panicked and being pissed off as he drove, he headed straight to her house.

All of the lights in the house appeared to be on and her car was there. Stepping onto the porch a twinge of uncomfortableness made him pause. He could hear music muffled by the house, coming from inside. What if she had company? He tried to shake the thought off, then laughed to himself as he decided, if he walked in on her getting down with some guy, it would be her fault for not sending a courtesy text. He leaned down, grabbed the spare key from inside a pair of cement boots that sat right next to the welcome mat, and unlocked the door. '21 Guns' by Green Day assaulted him the moment he opened the door. Now he had two missions.

"Liv!" he tried hollering over the music before deciding she would never hear him.
He could barely hear himself when he yelled.

Glaring at the closed door of the old marking room where Kieran had marked a lily on the left side of his chest, because sometimes, Braden really was a dumbass, he noticed the music wasn't as loud in the back of the house. Her bedroom door was cracked and the light was off. Leaning his head close to the opening, he listened for any extra sounds. If she was with someone and it was that quiet, the guy obviously wasn't doing a good job. Really, he'd be doing her a favor and as a reward he might 'accidentally' see her naked. Pushing the door open, he stepped in and found it empty.

Standing in Liv's dark and empty bedroom, he suddenly noticed how cold it was in the house. Where the hell was she? Sticking his hand in his pocket to give calling her another try, he came up empty and realized he'd left his cell phone in the car. Turning to walk out, he noticed something flash by the bathroom door. Making his way over, Braden saw a thick hot pink sweater and pair of jeans lying on the floor with her cell phone hanging out of the pocket.

Mission number two was accomplished as he picked up her phone and swiped her play list closed. The instant silence relaxed him. Until, he stepped into the bathroom and flipped the light on.

"Liv!" he blurted, seeing broken glass on the floor and her slumped over in the bathtub.

Her skin was blotchy and had a purple tint to it. With only her underwear, a black tank top and long socks that went to the bottom of her knees on, he started to feel sick. She was way too thin, making him wonder when was the last time she ate. How had anyone not noticed this? Crunching over the broken glass with his shoes, he crouched down and placed his hand on her shoulder. She was freezing. An empty bottle of Ever Clear rolled from her lap down her legs as he gave her a little shove.

"What are you doin' to yourself?" Braden questioned as she came to, reaching for the empty bottle.

Quickly pulling his hoodie off, he draped it over her back and around her shoulders.

Braden stood up and grabbed a towel off the rack before stepping to the side and laying it over the broken glass. Leaning back down, he pulled her up and out of the bathtub. Doing his best to carry her, as thin as she was, she was drunk, and a drunk person is nothing but dead weight. Her feet drug across the bathroom floor, until, they reached the carpet of her bedroom. He stopped for a moment to get a better hold on her. Heaving her into the air, he held her against himself as he walked her to the bed. After dropping her on her bed, Braden reached over to pull the comforter around her when he felt her pull the front of his shirt. Looking down at her, the light from the bathroom allowed him to see all the pain and anguish in her eyes.

"Braden," she breathed before tears rolled down her cheeks.

He was so stunned, it took him a minute to react. In all the years he'd know Liv, he'd never seen her even look like she might cry, not even at Kieran's funeral.

Pushing her farther onto the bed, Braden sat down, pulling Liv onto his lap and the comforter around them both. He wrapped his arms and legs around her trying to warm and sooth her at the same time as she curled up against him. Her body shook as she cried and he couldn't help the sting in his own eyes. For the first time in what seemed like forever, Braden felt like his life had meaning. He had a purpose.

1yr & 8 mo. Later...

Leaning back in his rolling desk chair, Braden shifted his feet, swaying himself from side to side. He didn't hate his job, but he didn't like it either. It could hardly be considered work, all he did was sit in his office and stare at the wall most of the day. Occasionally, he would print out a work order and take it to the warehouse supervisor. Aside from that, being the manager of Stockman's Superior Warehouse and Supply was no work at all. It was just a job. A place he went to five days a week, from nine to seven, in order to draw a paycheck.

At least it was Thursday, which meant he'd meet Liv out at the farmhouse right after work for beer and pizza night. It wasn't that he didn't enjoy going out or spending time with his girlfriend Mina, she was great, but Thursday nights with Liv were what he looked forward to the most each week. Those were the nights where he felt like he belonged. Mina never questioned his friendship with Liv, although he was sure she wanted to. She never pushed the issue though, and he was glad. For someone on the outside, it was more than likely hard to understand, Liv was a constant in his life.

They had, to be perfectly honest, Braden wasn't sure what they had. But it was deep, whatever it was. She saw past his ability to sabotage his own self and took pity on him when his heart was broken. In turn, he mourned for her when she was losing herself. There was no doubt in his mind that the heartaches and tragedies of life would have suffocated them both, had it not been for the connection they had with each other. While the world and everyone he knew was moving on, he was standing still and Liv was the only one right there beside him.

A tap on his office door pulled Braden away from his thoughts.

"My man." Pat, greeted, swinging the door open as he walked in.

Braden sat up and rolled himself back up to his desk.

Running his hand through his already slicked back dirty blonde hair, Pat shared, "Remember that deal I was telling you about?"

"The sure thing?" Braden replied, knowing it was bust just like every other risky venture his boss took.

"Yeah, well, turns out it wasn't as rock solid as I thought."

"Ya don't say." Braden patronized before asking, "How much did they get you for this time?"

With a smug expression, Pat assured, "My bank account is fine."

"But..."

"The company took a pretty big hit."

Shaking his head, Braden stood up, questioning, "How big?"

"Nothing I can't handle. I just need you to go lay off Pete."

"Pete from the warehouse? Why?"

Smiling as if he was a genius, Pat explained, "I did some figuring and the money I'll save by laying him off will cover the debt in six months."

"Didn't his wife just have a baby?"

"Twins. Last month."

Thinking this was low, even for Pat, Braden asked, "He'll get unemployment though, right?"

"For sure." Pat replied before laughing, "I mean he'll be lucky to get half of what he makes now but I'll rehire him as soon as all the money's put back."

"You can't do that." Braden snapped, irritated by his lack of thought for anyone other than himself.

Pat Stockman was a slick, fast talking, bigger better deal kind of guy. He always reminded Braden of a stereotypical used car salesman.

Although they were old friends, the term friend was used loosely. Very loosely. Pat always had big plans, or grand schemes depending on how you looked at it. He considered himself an entrepreneur but in reality he was more like a swindler. He spent most of his time, wheeling and dealing other peoples talents and skills for the right price.

Glaring at Braden, Pat took a step closer before running his hand through his hair again.

"I'm not. You are."

"Like hell I am." Braden argued.

"You still owe me."

Grimacing at the reminder, that Pat loved to throw in his face, Braden refused to back down.

"What you're doing is wrong. Why don't you not draw a salary and put the money back?"

"If you don't go give him the lay-off, I'll go fire him. The choice is yours, my friend."

Braden stared at him for a moment before offering, "I'll take the lay-off."

"You and Pete BFF's or somethin'? What's your problem?"

A moral call would be lost on Pat, so Braden decided to work and angle of his own.

"You're a business man, right?" Pat gave a suspicious nod as Braden continued, "If I take the lay-off, the money will get put back quicker and warehouse production won't be slowed down by losing Pete."

A wide smile spread across Pat's face as he agreed, "My man, that's why I like you."

Walking to the door, Braden asked, "It's a deal then?"

"Hey, you want to take one for the team. More power to you."

Giving Pat a short nod, he walked out of his office and down the hallway.

"Where are you going?"

"Didn't you hear, I just got laid-off." Braden sarcastically answered before heading out of the building.

~

Normally, Braden would have left straight from work and headed to Liv's but since she wouldn't be home for a few hours, he took the opportunity to pick up his clothes from Pheobe's Fluff and Fold laundry service and an eighteen pack of Dos Equis on his way to his apartment.

As soon as he walked in and set everything down on the couch, there was a knock on his door. When he opened it, Mina was right there on the other side with a soft smile.

Her brown eyes questioned him, while her mouth noted, "You're home early."

Opening the door wider to let her in, he replied, "I got laid-off."

"Oh no!" she blurted, swiftly turning around to face him as she walked in.

Closing the door, he assured, "It's not a big deal."

"My poor baby," she cooed, softly pressing her hands into his chest.

Braden considered the playful expression on her face, and hint of willingness in her eyes.

"It's okay, really," he replied, pulling his phone out of his pocket as it alerted him to a text with a light pinging sound.

Mina moved her hands from his chest and crossed them across her own, pouting, as he looked at his phone.

Biting the side of his tongue, Braden leaned his back against the door and smirked at his phone when he saw the text was from Liv.

L: Up for something new?

Glancing at Mina, he texted back.

B: Always.

L: Theme night.

B: Hope its Mexico. I already picked up Dos Equis.

L: Lucky Punk!

B: I'm gifted.

L: Ha! Later.

Laughing as he slid his phone back in his pocket, he noticed Mina wasn't humored at all.

"I'll just go so you can get ready."

"Don't be like that." Braden replied, gently wrapping his arms around her.

Shrugging in his arms, she stated, "I know tonight's her night with you."

"Do you have a problem with me and Liv?"

Mina's eyes softened as she shook her head, saying, "I'm not a jealous person. I just didn't realize that after almost a year with you, everything would still be the same as it was when we started dating."

"She's my friend." Braden shared, wondering why suddenly his Thursday night tradition was an issue.

Pretending like she hadn't just suggested he stop going to Liv's, Mina replied, "I know."

Slightly confused, he questioned, "So?"

"So you're just going to have to kiss me good enough to tide me over until tomorrow," she advised, pressing herself into him as she waited for him to comply.

Her lips were soft and warm as they moved effortlessly with his kiss.

Mina was sweet and kind, not to mention beautiful. She had big brown eyes and long brown hair that curled naturally against the sides of her face. Her body was lean and fit from her morning trips to the gym before work at the hospital. Admittedly he was attracted to women curvier than Mina, but what she lacked in curves she more than made up for in flexibility. What he liked about her most of all was that she was easy. Not in a sexual way, although he didn't exactly have to work for it, it was her personality. She was easy going. He wasn't in love but caring about her seemed to come as second nature to him. Everything with Mina was effortless.

A slight giggle caused Braden to break their kiss and give Mina a questioning look.

With an excited expression, she cheered, "I was just thinking, she can have you on Thursday's because now that you're laid-off and my rounds end at noon, we'll get to see each other every single day." He stared at her as she continued. "And, if your lay-off lasts too long, we can share an apartment."

Braden started to respond but didn't get the chance. She leaned forward and gave him a quick kiss on the cheek. Wearing a wide smile she flicked her finger down the end of his nose and bounced out of his apartment.

Braden stood there for a moment wondering if it was just him, or was that entire conversation incredibly strange. Shaking it off, he grabbed the beer off of the couch and set it in the freezer before taking his laundry with him to his room.

~

On the way to Liv's, Braden couldn't help thinking about his conversation with Mina. A 'relationship' talk was yet to take place between them, other than the few times she asked if he was seeing anyone else. He wasn't and her constant enthusiasm led him to believe she wasn't either. Since he had decided, after things finally ended with his ex-girlfriend Lily, a serious relationship wasn't for him, he never put too much thought into it. After all, how could he, when he already wore another woman's mark.

When he arrived at Liv's she was in the kitchen, swaying in front of her stove, moving her head and shoulders to the music only she could hear. Before he made it to the refrigerator, she turned and smirked at the eighteen-pack he was carrying. He flashed a wide grin at her and nodded before continuing to the fridge.

That's how it was between them. They talked to each other, but sometimes it was unnecessary. Most of the time, he knew what she was thinking and it was the same for her. From the time that their friendship developed, Braden never stopped appreciating her. Mostly because he felt like no one else truly did. Penny, Charlotte, Seth and Auggie loved her of course, but they didn't see her like he did. And his cousin, Kieran who died without realizing how lucky he was to have her as his wife sure as hell didn't. It was the little things like a few years ago when she instituted beer and pizza night. Wearing wireless earbuds, because she hated quiet but knew hearing music in the house upset him, and her almost brutal honesty, in every situation. If she had something to say, she never held back. Liv was the most upfront person he'd ever known.

Braden grabbed two beers and set them to the side before placing the other sixteen on the bottom shelf of Liv's refrigerator.

Walking past him, Liv shared, "Pizza's almost ready."

"Are you seeing anyone?"

Turning to him, she gave a curious look, "Is that your business?"

Handing her a beer, Braden replied, "You know what I realized today?"

"That you're not as involved with my personal life as you'd like to be?" she asked with a smirk.

Braden rolled his eyes and laughed before sharing, "Mina and I have been dating for almost a year.

"You just realized that?"

"When she said, 'We've been dating for almost a year,' I did."

"Ha!" she blurted before informing, "Some boyfriend you are."

"Right?"

Braden started to laugh, then stopped as Liv's expression grew serious.

"You wantin' to bail on Thursdays?"

He gave a half-hearted smile noticing the apprehension in her blue eyes.

"No."

With a suspicious tone, she questioned, "You sure?"

Knowing Thursdays were the only thing in his life he was sure about, Braden nodded.

Liv continued to stare at him as she took the blue tooth earbuds out of her ears.

"If I was her, I wouldn't want you coming here."

Raising his eyebrows at her, Braden asked, "If you were seeing someone, would you let him come between us?"

Her expression instantly changed as she let out a loud, "Ha!" and laughed, "You're not putting your commitment issues on me."

Placing his hand across his chest Braden gave a wide smile as he swore, "Hey, I'm committed to beer and pizza."

"Yeah, you have issues," she laughed, turning as the oven timer went off.

~

After Liv won all seven rounds of Loteria, her Mexican Bingo game, the pizza was gone and so was all of the beer.

She was collecting the cards and placing them back in the box teasing, "Maybe one day," before laughing, "Ha! Just kidding, I always win."

"You suck." Braden griped as he cleared their plates and empty bottles off of the table.

"Awe, don't be a sore loser," she replied before picking up her game, taunting, "You should be used to it by now," as she sashayed out of the kitchen.

Braden watched her victory walk until she disappeared down the hallway that led to her bedroom.

Sitting quietly on the ottoman, Liv hesitated. Braden was asleep on the couch in front of her. She knew she needed to wake him but he seemed so at peace with himself, she waited. Watching his chest rise and fall as he slept, she caught herself keeping rhythm with his breath. As each inhale and exhale passed perfectly in sync with his, Liv closed her eyes.

Their friendship, while unusual to most everyone around them, gave her purpose. She had been in love twice in her life and both times she had been hurt. Her relationship with Braden wasn't love. It was hard to explain. On the outside everyone saw only what they wanted them to see. Braden and Liv knew each other on the inside. She had watched him break just like he had seen her unravel and somehow for a few hours each Thursday night between the board games and beer, they were whole again.

As Liv slowly opened her eyes, she felt herself smile.

Hopping up from the ottoman, she clapped her hands just inches from Braden's face while alerting, "Wake Up!"

Groaning, he rolled over, putting his back to her.

"Come on, punk, get up. You're going to be late for work."

"I got laid-off yesterday," he replied, his voice muffled by the couch cushions.

"That sucks. You hungry?"

Rolling onto his back, Braden looked up at her.

"Bacon and eggs?"

Turning to walk out of the living room, Liv asked, "Are you going to start looking for another job?"

Braden let out a loud yawn as he stood, following her to the kitchen.

"Nah, I think I'll be alright. I have some money saved and I'm going to file for unemployment."

Pulling a package of bacon and a carton of eggs out of the refrigerator and setting them on the counter by the stove, she offered, "If you run short, I've got some work around here."

"Whatcha need?"

Liv unwrapped the bacon and dropped it in the skillet as Braden leaned against the counter next to her.

"I'm turning Kieran's marking room into a library."

"You are?"

Nodding, she started to explain, "This book I read a few months ago, said..."

Braden cut her off, laughing, "You and your self-help books."

"It was an erotic thriller that centered around..."

"Hold on," he interrupted her again, "Erotic like porn?"

Shrugging her shoulder as she poked at the bacon with a fork, Liv clarified, "More like mystery with lots of hot sex."

"You dirty girl," he teased with a wide smile before questioning, "So this 'library' you're wantin', is really a room to stash your porn collection?"

"No, I keep all the porn on my kindle in the drawer next to my bed." Liv replied with a smirk. Braden started to smile then narrowed his eyes at her. Instinctively, she narrowed her eyes back at him, without realizing they were having a stand off until he broke into a full sprint towards the back of the house. Quickly removing the skillet from the burner before turning it off, Liv rushed to the back, after him.

By the time she made it into the room, Braden had her kindle in one hand, swiping pages with the other.

"Here we go," he announced as something apparently caught his eye. "Roughly rubbing circles around her..."

"Put it down," she snapped, marching towards him.

Backing into the corner, he skipped to, "Threading his fingers into the back of her hair, he pulled her down to his aching..."

Reaching to snatch her kindle from him, she blurted, "Damn it!" As he held it high above his head, exclaiming, "Wait! This part's highlighted!"

"Give it here, punk!" Liv practically growled, pulling at his sleeve until they both heard the material start to tear.

Finally giving in, Braden said, "Alright. Geez." Lowering his arm and handing it back to her.

Grabbing it out of his hand, she set her kindle back in her open drawer and slammed it shut.

Slightly out of breath, she glared at him.

"Guess that answers the question of, 'Are you seeing anyone?'" he teased with a laugh.

"Or maybe I like to try new things."

All humor left his expression as he stood there staring at her.

"Nuh-uh..."

Liv smiled, arching an eyebrow at him as she replied, "Thursday's only one night. You really think I sit here alone every other night reading?"

Braden looked at the floor, mumbling, "I don't know."

Without waiting for him to look back up at her, Liv turned and walked out of the room.

~

Driving to work, Liv wasn't embarrassed by what Braden read on her kindle, she was more offended than anything. Even if it was true, he had no right to assume she was spending every night alone. Besides, if anyone deserved a wild adventurous sex life, it was her. That type of life had been non-existent long before her husband died. Not to mention, the only two men she had slept with, one in high school and the other she married, both lost interest in her.

Her first time was a one night stand with her high school crush. It was almost understandable that by the very next day he had forgotten all about her. Seeing as she had never even spoken to him before handing her virginity over to him one night.

Kieran though, she never quite understood. He was her husband. A man she committed her life to. The one that when they were dating, swore she was the sexiest woman he'd seen in his entire life. Slowly, within the bonds of marriage, their sex life suffered. Until one day, it stopped all together.

With that in mind, Liv felt she needed to prove something to herself. She wasn't looking to just have sex, otherwise she'd already be doing it. Love wasn't a part of the equation either. What she wanted was passion, all-consuming hunger for another person, and a moment where she could see nothing but desire for her in a man's eyes. That's what she wanted.

Strolling into Legacy Ink, Liv gave Jimmy a short wave on her way to the back. Jimmy was an old high school buddy of Kieran's who for years just hung around the shop talking mess and hitting on every girl that walked into the shop. Once Liv took over the tattoo shop and made Penny a partner, she decided if Jimmy was there all day anyway they might as well get some use out of him. He wasn't the brightest but he could schedule appointments. Not only did hiring him take some of the burden off Penny and Liv with the shops growing popularity, he was their security too. Everyone in town knew him and were not likely to start anything that he would need to finish. Those who came from out of town would see a six foot four mass of muscles and tattoos as soon as they walked into the shop. It was a smart decision to hire him.

After tossing her purse on a chair in the small make shift office in the back, Liv walked back to the front.

"What's the day look like?" she asked, making her way up to the counter.

Jimmy glanced over the calendar and replied, "One this afternoon. I thought Penny needed a break. She's booked solid everyday next week."

Rubbing her hands together, Liv nodded, saying, "We really need to get someone else in here. She's gonna end up with arthritis or some kinda hand disfigurement if this keeps up."

"Want me to put an ad online?"

"Not yet, but maybe soon." Liv answered, turning when the bell above the shop door rang.
A twinge of excitement nudged a smile that she promptly held back, as the door closed behind a man with dirty blonde slicked back hair and a brown leather jacket.

Jimmy mumbled something under his breath as Liv stepped away from the counter.

"What's up, Pat?" she greeted.

"Everything, lookin' at you, Liv."
Liv stared at him in response, giving the impression she was unimpressed.

Keeping his focus on Liv, Pat asked, "How goes it, Jimmy?"

"Pat." Jimmy replied in a flat tone.

With a sarcastic smile, Liv stated, "Since its obvious we all know each other's names, you can step to the back with me."
Pat happily obliged, following behind her as she headed back to the office.

Feeling his eyes on her as she walked, Liv took her time making it the short distance to the back room.

"Invoice?" She questioned, holding her hand out to him.

Patting his hands down his chest and torso, he replied, "Guess I forgot it."

"You must not want to get paid then," she assured, crossing her arms in front of her chest.

"Tell you what, spend the night with me and we'll call it even."

"Know what that's called?"

"It's called a trade, baby, and I'm all about the barter system."

"My ass isn't up for negotiation." Liv spouted, brushing past him as she headed out of the room. Pat circled his arms around her waist, pulling her back into the room to face him.

"You know I enjoy this little back and forth thing we do, but sooner or later you're gonna give in."

Liv allowed him to keep his arms around her as she questioned, "Pretty cocky there?"

Reaching around to swing the door closed, he offered, "Wanna see for yourself?"

"You wish," she laughed, pressing against him.

"I do." Pat replied before leaning in saying, "You're hard on the outside with your tattoos and bad attitude but I bet you're soft and warm on the inside."

Tilting her chin up, Liv invited his kiss.

Liv had known Pat for years. She even went out with him a few times before she met Kieran at one of his parties. He wasn't exactly trustworthy though, and she knew most of his business practices were shady. However, there was an undeniable attraction when it came to Pat, one that was never going to move past making out in the back of the shop every so often. But still, it was something tangible that made her feel like a woman and that in itself was reason enough to keep it going.

While his hands roamed the front of her clingy t-shirt, his lips glided softly against hers.

With a deep breath, Pat pulled away, swearing, "You know, it's gonna take me a good hour to come down from this."

"Best get on with the recovery process then."

Pat gave a slight laugh and kissed her again before saying, "You say the sweetest things to me."

Liv winked at him with a smirk on her face as she motioned towards the door.

"Admit it. I'm wearing you down."

Snapping her fingers, she pointed at him, declaring, "Keep hope alive."

Shaking his head with a smile, Pat walked out of the room.

Focusing on her lips in the small rectangular mirror on the wall as she reapplied her lipstick, Liv waited to hear the bell above the door ring before stepping out of the back.

"You can do better." Jimmy griped as she walked past him.

"I'm not doing him."

"I figured, since he keeps comin' back."

Turning back to him, she shot him a questioning glare.

"And word has it he's quick on the draw, without packin' a whole lot."

"That's the word, huh?"

Jimmy's expression was dead serious as he nodded, causing Liv to laugh at his way of being a friend to her.

Braden was expecting a much larger crowd when he walked into The Dog House late Saturday night. It was usually packed. He preferred it that way. When the bar was full it was easy to ignore the music inside. Tonight, with little chatter from the handful of customers he could hear 'The Man Who Broke His Own Heart' by Everclear playing throughout the bar.

A pint of Guinness and an empty stool were waiting on him when he reached the bar.

"You scare off all the customers?"

Auggie gave a hard scowl before running his hand down the front of his red beard.

"They all heard you were comin' and left."

Braden lifted his beer, taking a long sip before smiling, "How's it goin', brother?"

"Can't complain. You?"

"All good here." Braden answered, taking another sip of beer before Penny, slid onto the barstool next to him.

"Where's Mina?"

Glancing behind his sister to give her husband Seth a nod, Braden replied, "A friend of hers needed the night off so she picked up her shift."

Penny smiled wide as she cheered, "She's so sweet. Are y'all getting serious? Y'all have been dating for almost a year now."

Wondering why everyone was suddenly bringing up their dating time span, he shrugged and shook his head before returning his focus to the beer in front of him.

The fact that the song playing overhead switched to 'Believe' by Mumford & Sons, mixed with the inquisitive stares of all three of them, gave Braden and uneasy feeling. So much so, that when Charlotte, Auggie's wife, made her way behind the bar with her blonde hair pulled into a loose ponytail, he grabbed his half full pint of Guinness and downed it in one gulp. Turning away from the bar, he was prepared to walk out and let them judge him behind his back, when a familiar face caught his eye.

It took a minute of staring before Braden could admit to himself that what he was seeing was real.

"Looks like Pat's still trying to 'collect' on that invoice." Charlotte remarked as Penny giggled at what must have been and inside joke between the two of them. Braden didn't find it funny.

Without taking his eyes off Liv, he questioned, "From the chairs at the shop? That was three months ago. Why hasn't she paid it?"

"I don't think he wants her to." Charlotte replied before Penny shared, "He comes into the shop every once and a while. They always go to the back so she can write him a check, then...um... he says he forgot to bring the invoice."

In Braden's mind, the rational explanation was that of course he was hitting on her. Surely, she would give him hell for it before letting him go.

That was until Penny continued, "I don't know what they do back there, but she's always in a real good mood for the rest of the day after he leaves." Uneasy was now an understatement as Braden watched as Liv allowed Pat to run the palm of his hand slowly up and down the tattoos on her arm.

"I think it's good, she needs..." Charlotte started to say before he cut her off, snapping, "He's not good for her. He's... Not good for her." Unable to take any more of the situation in, Braden pushed away from the bar and walked out.

He only made it a few steps out of the doors before Seth stopped him.

"Hey, wait up."

Shaking his head Braden turned to Seth, venting, "Out of everybody in this damn town, that's who she picks to hook up with?"

"Instead of you?" Seth asked in a cautious yet serious tone.

"You know I'm not into her like that."

Seth's expression bordered on disbelief as he suggested, "I think you might like her more than you're willing to admit."

"Nah, man. I mean if one night she wanted to play naked twister I'd be all in, but I don't think about her like that."

"Never?"

Braden paused for a moment to think before answering, "I'm a guy. I know what she looks like but I don't dwell on it because...there's more to her than that."

"And you don't think that's reason enough?"

Disliking being put on the spot, Braden replied, "I think I have a girlfriend."

"Mina? The girl, who after almost a year, everyone loves but you?"

Surprised at how outspoken Seth was being, he questioned, "Why are you so interested in what I've got going on?"

With a loud exhale, he confessed, "Penny's making me crazy."

Wanting to laugh, the look on Seth's face was so sincere Braden held back.

Seth paced back and forth for a moment before settling in one spot.

"I look at her and she just seems like she would be fertile."

"What now?" Braden questioned, thinking he must have misunderstood.

Shaking his head at himself, Seth continued, "I was excited. I've been thinking about her having my babies since before the first time we slept together."

Braden started to glare at his brother in law, but allowed him to continue.

"At first it was great. I could barely keep her off of me to go to work, but now she's got these designated sex days that coincide with her ovulation..."

Holding his hand up, Braden had to stop him, "You know that's my sister, right?"

Appearing genuinely regretful, Seth replied, "I'm sorry. I know, but she's crazy."

Braden patted him on the back, reminding, "She's a Caffrey. You were warned."

Taking a deep breath, Seth nodded.

"Come on, let's go back in and get you a beer."

Jumping back a little, Seth exclaimed, "That's another thing! I'm only allowed one beer a week!"

"That's insane!"

Seth appeared serious as a heart attack as he declared, "The struggle is real."

Laughing out loud, Braden followed Seth back into The Dog House.

It wasn't long after they were back inside that Liv joined them at the bar.

Braden tried to block out what he had seen earlier but couldn't as he blurted, "I thought you were on a date," earning a disapproving expression from everyone, including Liv.

She narrowed her eyes at him for a minute longer than everyone else before announcing, "Did y'all hear? This one's gonna be my man servant," pointing her thumb at Braden.

"Your what?" Braden choked, almost spitting his sip of beer everywhere.

Ignoring his question, she continued, "Now I don't have to worry about hiring a stranger that'll go through my stuff."

"I would've come out there if you needed something fixed." Auggie informed.

With a light smile, she nodded, "I know but he doesn't have anything better to do."

"You know I'm sitting right here." Braden griped as they continued to talk as if he wasn't there.

"You should make him wear an outfit." Charlotte advised.

Auggie scowled at his wife as Penny wrinkled up her nose and shook her head.

"Come on, if the situation was reversed you know Braden would try to get her to wear one of those frilly maid dresses."

"True." Liv agreed before questioning, "What's the guy version of that?"

Penny's eyes suddenly went wide as Seth replied, "Penny likes naked."

Scowling at Seth, Auggie stepped away to fill a drink order, while Liv gave a loud, "Ha!" and Charlotte said, "Well, oh-kay..."

"I like my man Seth's idea." Braden replied, flashing a smile at Liv.

"No." Liv stated, pointing a finger directly at him.

Charlotte smiled, suggesting, "Suits are sexy. I love when Auggie wears one. He's all scruffy and polished at the same time." Then looking Braden over she added, "But you're kinda pretty so, that might not work."

"Ya know, he is kinda pretty." Auggie shared, back in the conversation.

"Maybe I should get you a frilly maid outfit then." Liv smirked at him.

Penny pursed her lips into a smile as she swept her long auburn hair over her shoulder, teasing, "I've always been jealous."

Seth remarked, "He really is."

"Thanks, man." Braden replied, thinking at least Seth would have had his back.

"Hey, I said Penny and naked in the same sentence. I'm lucky to still be alive at this point." At that moment, even Auggie couldn't help but laugh.

When the night came to an end Braden ended up with a hard buzz from several pints of beer, and a ride home from Liv. Crossing his arms against his chest, in the passenger seat of her Dodge Challenger HellCat, he worked at focusing his attention on the road ahead. Although he appreciated the silence, it was starting to feel uncomfortable.

Leaning his head in her direction, Braden said, "You are seeing someone."
Liv responded with a slight frown, but didn't reply.

"Why Pat?"
Shaking her head, she remained silent.

"You won't answer me 'cause you know the kinda person he is."

As soon as they came to the red light, Liv stopped the car and looked directly at him, "Didn't I tell you who I see is none of your business."

Making a disgusted sound he shared, "I would never get with someone you disapproved of."

Glaring at him she stated, "Lily," then turned away, staring straight ahead.
The second the light turned green, she sped off down the road.

No matter how much he wanted to, there was not a thing more he could say. Liv's detest for Lily had been made clear long before she and Braden were friends. He never knew why she disliked her so much, but by the time it was finally over between them every single member of his family did too.

Liv pulled into a parking spot right in front of his apartment. He knew she was angry with him because he heard the doors unlock as she shifted her car into reverse.

"I don't like it when you're pissed at me." Braden shared, remaining seated with no intention of getting out of her car.

Keeping the car in reverse, she revved her engine with her foot planted against the break.

"You don't like it either."

Liv's arms tensed as she gripped the steering wheel and closed her eyes, demanding, "Get out of my car."

Holding back a smile, he coaxed, "Not until you say you're not mad."

Shifting her car into park, she turned and looked at him, saying, "You're like a damn kid."

"I'm older than you."

With a slight smirk, she assured, "It doesn't seem like it. You still dress like a sixteen year old boy."

After glancing down at his faded jeans and Vans, he looked over at her black and white Converse, dark jeans and Ramones T-shirt.

"So do you."

Liv let out a laugh before shaking her head at him saying, "Come on. Its late and I'm tired."

"You wanna stay over?"

Braden noticed a confused expression fall across her face, as if she didn't know how to answer.

"Do you?"

Looking away from him, she replied, "Mina."

"She won't care. I stay at your house all the time."

Shaking her head at him, Liv pointed towards the windshield, saying, "No. Mina."

Braden looked out seeing his girlfriend waving at them with an interested yet sweet expression across her face.

"See you Monday then."

With a nod, Liv shifted her car back into reverse.

Stumbling a little as he got out of Liv's car, Braden barely closed the door when Mina was right there by his side. Wrapping her arms around his shoulders, she pressed up against him.

"I missed you."

Braden waited for Liv's car to pull out of the parking spot before leaning down to kiss her.

~

Flipping the lights on in the living room, Liv swiped the playlist open on her phone at the same time. 'Back To The Shack' by Weezer instantly thundered through her house bringing a smile to her face. The disruption of silence in her house paused for a second as text flashed across her cell.

B: You make it home okay?

She found it odd that Braden was texting her. He seemed pretty invested in Mina when she dropped him off.

L: Safe and sound.

B: OK

Even though it was a simple text, it didn't feel right.

L: You okay?

Waiting for his response, her phone rang.

"What's up?" Liv asked, answering Braden's call.

His tone was flat as he replied, "Nothin'."

"You havin' some sort of a moment?"

There was a long pause before he replied, "I'm just drunk."

"Probably," she replied without knowing the issue, but recalling he had about seven pints at the bar.

"'Night."

"Later." Liv replied before ending the call.

Walking to her bedroom, she considered calling Pat and taking him up on his offer.

She was surprised to see him at The Dog House and even more surprised that he was flirting with her there. The anticipation of him standing close, wondering how far he was willing to go in public excited her. Then he gave her that inviting smile he slid his hand down her arm. It was such a high, until she glanced towards the bar and saw Auggie scowling at her.

By the time she made it to her room and looked at her bed, she changed her mind. She knew there was no reason to feel guilty but how could she help it. Her husband's death had done nothing to remove him from her life. It simply made her feel even more alone. Over two years had gone by and she couldn't even bring herself to spend the night at Braden's. Thursday night had been an institution long before his death, but staying the night in another man's home, even his, was completely different. Though she had moments of freedom where there was physical thought or action with no emotion involved, Liv couldn't let go long enough for anything real. It was a painfully agonizing feeling to know what she wanted and needed, and at the same time riddled with doubt and disbelief that it was a possibility. That was where she and Braden differed. He was able to move on. Not fully and be complete as a whole, but in a physical way. Liv envied that about him. The damage Lily had done scared him in so many ways beyond repair, but sex wasn't one of the losses of being with her.

As she laid across her bed, Liv reflected back on the last time she and Kieran were together. It had been months since they were intimate and after trying everything she could think of to get him interested in her, she decided an out of character for her, sexy dress and heels at Charlotte and Auggie's wedding might do the trick. Initially, it worked. He couldn't keep his hands off her. They didn't even make it all the way to the house. Pulling off on an old dead end dirt road on the way home, he swore he couldn't wait a second more. In the moment, she felt wild, alive, and desired. Unfortunately, making it home wasn't the only thing he couldn't wait for, leaving her feeling empty, used and unsatisfied. Still thinking it was a start, the promise of rekindling their relationship soon vanished as he fell right back into ignoring her the very next day.

She once considered turning Kieran's marking room into sex room as her way of giving his deceased ass the finger, but aside from the fact that that would require her having sex, it was just a little way to make herself feel like she had some control over what was happening. She didn't though. Liv was just as hurt as she was when he was alive. Except with him gone, the wound would never heal.

Dragging himself off his couch, Braden went down on his knees on the carpet before pushing up on the couch cushions to stand. He rubbed his eyes, staggering toward his apartment door to see who was banging on it. Peering out of the peephole, he rubbed his eyes hard and looked again. Stepping back and cursing under his breath, he ran his fingers through his hair in an attempt to look presentable.

On the other side of his door stood a medium height older woman with auburn hair pulled into a long braid and lips pursed up into a somewhat judgmental forced smile.

"Hey... Mom," he greeted, leaning forward to hug her.

Sarah leaned away, fussing, "When was the last time you showered."

Running his hands down the front of his t-shirt, Braden stepped back and let his mom in.

"I swear, son. This is a pig sty," she declared the moment she stepped in.

Flashing her a quick smile, he wrapped an arm around her, suggesting, "You always said, *if you can't do something right, don't do it at all*."

"Go clean yourself up." Sarah ordered, pushing him away from her.

Watching his mom immediately start picking up on her way to the kitchen, Braden hurried to his room to take a quick shower.

He was still a bit hungover but having his apartment cleaned up and possibly a home cooked breakfast was already making him feel better.

Rounding the corner into the kitchen, he asked, "Were ya missing your favorite son?"

Without looking up from the dishes, she replied, "I'm worried about your sister."

"And seeing me makes you feel better?" Braden joked with a wide smile.

Giving him a sideways glance, Sarah stated, "I think there's something wrong with her. She should be pregnant by now."

"Mom..." he started before hearing a knock at his door.

As he made his way to see who was at the door, his mom continued, "I'm not sure they're trying hard enough. Or they're not doing it right."

Braden swung the door open in hopes someone was there to save him from a conversation, he did not want to have.

"Hi." Mina cheered, causing him to regret opening it.

This was going to be worse than the Penny fertility conversation.

Braden pulled the door closed until only his head was sticking out of the doorway.

"Can you come back later?" he urged with a weak smile.

Just as she started to pout, they both heard Sarah gripe, "Son, are you listening?"

Mina's face instantly lit up as she blurted, "Son? Your mom's here?"

As the idea of shutting the door in her face started sounding better and better, Sarah walked up beside him and pulled it open.

"Girlfriend?"

Stepping into his apartment, Mina replied, "Yes, ma'am. I'm Mina."

Sarah eyed her suspiciously before acknowledging, "The nurse, right?"

Glancing back at Braden with a smile of wonder, like he was the one that shared information about her with his mom, she nodded.

"Shouldn't Penny already be pregnant?"

Caught off guard, Mina questioned, "Ma'am?

"You're a nurse." Sarah stated, putting her on the spot.

Stepping to the side Braden smiled to himself thinking, bet your real excited to meet her now.

Mina was quiet for a moment before replying, "Well, Mrs. Caffrey, there are many factors that can delay conception for couples that are trying to conceive."

Pleasantly surprised, Sarah led her to the kitchen table. As they both sat and started discussing birth control and menstrual cycles Braden wondered if he would ever be able to eat at his table again.

Five minutes into hearing things he never wanted to and could never un-hear, Braden had to get out of there.

"I'll be right back."

Before either of them had a chance to look up, he was out of the door and in front of his apartment.

"What's up, punk?" Liv greeted as she walked up.

Braden couldn't believe his luck as he replied, "You're awesome!"

"Yeah," she agreed with a smirk before saying, "You wanna go get your car or what?"

"Yes!" he exclaimed almost jumping up and down.

Liv gave him a strange look as he motioned for her to follow him.

"Who's in there?"

Biting the side of his tongue, he smiled before confessing, "Mina and my mom."

"Ha!"

"Don't laugh. They're in there talking about Penny's cycles and ovaries."

Letting out a loud breath of air, Liv walked past him and into his apartment.

Stepping in as if she owned the room, Liv pulled out the chair in between Mina and Sarah.

Batting her eyes, she gave a wide smile almost singing, "Hi, Sarah," then turned to Mina and saying, "Hello."

Sarah sighed as she replied, "Liv."

"So what's the kitchen table convo?"

Mina perked up, smiling as she shared, "I was just telling Mrs. Caffrey, Penny's trouble with getting pregnant..."

Braden noticed his mom give Mina a 'shut your mouth' glare as Liv asked, "You and Penny are good friends?"

Nodding, Mina replied, "She's super sweet."

"So, she asked you to talk to her mom about her troubles?"

Mina appeared confused as she stuttered, "No... Well... I..."

With a quick nod, Liv turned to Sarah, saying, "I see, Penny asked you to ask her brother's girlfriend why she wasn't pregnant yet?"

"She was being helpful." Sarah snapped as Liv stood back up.

"That's good 'cause something that private could really hurt someone's feelings, ya know." Mina looked down at the table with an embarrassed expression.

"Why are you here, Liv?" Sarah griped, clearly feeling the sting of Liv's insinuation also.

"This one was too drunk to drive home last night," she replied, pointing at Braden.

Throwing his hands out in front of him, Braden was shocked.

"Braden Hagen Caffrey!" Sarah yelled directly at him before Liv added, "It's cool, he got laid-off so it's not like he has anything else to do."

Sarah looked like she was about to jump out of her chair and smack Braden, as he stood there with his mouth hanging open.

"We still gettin' your car?" Liv asked, glancing at Braden as she turned and walked out. Braden knew his mom was about to let him have it. Weighing his options, he rushed out of his apartment after Liv.

Swiftly following her to her car, Braden knew she was mad but didn't understand why he had fallen into the line of her fire.

He slid into the passenger seat griping, "What the hell?" As Liv started her car, revving the engine, and drowning out the sound of his voice.

Liv backed out of the parking spot, shifted into drive, and took off, assuring, "You're lucky I didn't leave your ass there."

"What did I do?"

Slamming on her breaks, jerking them both forward at the stop sign, she fussed, "You know damn good and well Penny's feelings would be hurt if she knew they were talking about her. She's had your back so many times, you should've never let that conversation happen."

"'Cause my mom's gonna listen to anything I have to say?" he snapped back at her.

"No, but your girlfriend would have."

Her words made him feel uneasy as he argued, "Mina's a nurse. She was just tryin' to be helpful."

"Yeah? Or was she tryin' to get in good with Sarah?"

Liv's question instantly silenced Braden as he realized, he wasn't sure.

After rolling through the stop sign, neither said a word until Liv pulled beside Braden's El Camino in front of The Dog House.

"Sorry."

Shifting into park, Liv turned to him.

"Ha! Your dumbass sure will be when you get back."

Braden stared at her for a minute.

Shaking his head at himself as he realized he left his overly eager girlfriend sitting with his mom at his apartment, he mumbled, "What was I thinking?"

Liv took a moment to laugh at him before questioning, "What's your deal with her anyway?"

"What do you mean?"

Giving him a look of 'you know exactly what I mean,' Liv sat there waiting for his answer.

Shrugging, Braden leaned his head back against the headrest, saying, "She's easy to be with."

"If you say so."

Opening the passenger door, he gave her a questioning look.

With an air of wisdom, Liv stated, "For something you claim is so easy, it sure comes off as forced."

"What about you and Pat?" Braden asked, trying to take the focus off of how her advice made him feel.

Liv frowned, sharing, "I'm not with him."

"Do you wanna be?"

With a slight smirk, she replied, "Not a conversation I'm gonna have with you."

"Why? I'll tell you anything you want to know about me and Mina."

Liv quickly shifted her car into reverse, assuring, "No thanks. I've got Charlotte if I wanna have a sex talk."

Shaking his head with a laugh, Braden got out of her car and closed the door.

Driving back to his apartment, it took a little while for what Liv said to register. He almost had to pull over on the side of the road when it hit him that she wasn't interested in dating Pat. Suddenly the things he'd read on her kindle bombarded his mind. It wasn't like he thought she should go join a convent or even abstain from anything, he just didn't really think about her having sex. Now he was. Braden was thinking about Liv having sex, and with Pat of all people.

Wiping off a storage bin as she set it on the dolly, Liv forgot how much of her belongings she stored out in the old shed when she first moved into the farmhouse with Kieran. She had already managed to get three of the plastic tubs into the house. One was on her dolly, and there were still four stacked in the corner of the shed. Looking at her dusty rag, she tossed it down and wiped her forehead off with the back of her hand. Ten thirty in the morning was definitely too early to break a sweat. Hearing Braden's car pull onto her gravel driveway, Liv blew out a loud breath. She twisted her hair into a knot above her head and walked out of the shed.

Liv stood in front of his car as it came to a stop.

"Can you believe how hot it is," she griped as Braden got out of his car.

Shaking his head with a laugh, he replied, "It's only eighty."

Continuing to hold her hair on the top of her head, Liv wiped down the side of her face and neck with her free hand, saying, "At ten in the morning, in December."

"What were you doing?"

Turning to walk back to the shed, she replied, "Digging my stuff out."

"You couldn't wait for me?"

Liv picked up her pace, saying, "There's more than I remembered."

She dropped her hair, feeling as though holding onto it was slowing her down. When Braden caught up with her, she increased her pace a little more.

"Hey," he said with humor in his voice.

"Yeah?"

"Are you trying to beat me to the shed?"

"Ha!" she blurted before taking three long strides and stepping past the doors, assuring, "There was no trying to it."

"You have issues," he laughed before picking the storage bin up off of the dolly and carrying it out of the shed.

Dusting off the last four bins, Liv couldn't help watching Braden from the corner of her eye as he lifted each one and carried it out of the shed. This may have been a bad idea. Thursday nights were sacred, but outside the sanctity of that one night a week, they were never alone together. Aside from the next morning, and car ride here and there, Liv had kept it that way on purpose. As much as she wanted to deny it, it was never Pat that she thought about, even when she was letting him feel her up.

Liv turned as Braden carried the last bin out of the shed. Following him into the house she needed to give him the list of things she wanted done, shower and go to work.

Placing the storage bin he was carrying with the others in the old marking room, Braden complained, "What the hell is in these?"

Standing in the doorway, Liv replied, "Mostly books."

Wiping his forearm across his forehead, he said, "Damn they were heavy." Before adding, "Now I'm sweatin'," as he started to pull his shirt off.

Liv's stomach instantly lurched in panic as she held out her hand and blurted, "Don't."
With his arms crossed in front of his torso, he held the sides of his shirt and smiled.

"Worried Pat might get jealous?"

"I just don't wanna see your badge of honor that's all," she replied with a smirk.
Liv knew what the lily her husband tattooed on the left side of Braden's chest looked like, she didn't need or want to see it permanently marked on his skin.

"What's the matter? It's just a little ink," he teased with a hint of irritation.
That mark, the one Kieran betrayed his legacy with, had already caused enough hurt and done enough damage for her to know that wasn't true.

Before she knew it, the words, "Don't start talking shit because you were too much of a dumbass to realize she never loved you," flew form her mouth.

Braden froze. There was so much hurt in his eyes, it wounded her at the same time.

"Screw you, Liv." Braden grumbled, brushing past her as he walked out of the room.

Closing her eyes, she balled her fists, blew out a loud breath, and followed him.

Braden was pouring himself a glass of water when she walked into the kitchen. This was another reason why spending extra time with him was a bad idea. There were things that would eventually come up that had no business being discussed. Regardless, at the moment, this was on her. While what she said was true, it never should have been said, especially by her.

Stepping in front of him, Liv assured, "That was an asshole thing to say."

"Yeah, it was," he replied with anger in his voice as he continued to drink his water.

Knowing she was in the wrong by allowing the hurt someone else had caused her to backlash onto him, as if the situation hadn't hurt him enough all on its own. Liv waited until he set his glass down. Allowing her guard to slip just enough to be sincere, she stepped closer, and covered his fist that was clinched on the counter with her hand. Staring into his brown eyes, that she always thought should have been green, Liv let her eyes emphasize the sorry her words could not express.

Braden was silent as he wrinkled his brow in response. He searched her eyes before relenting to her unspoken apology. Liv continued to stare at him as he broke eye contact and looked down at their hands. She felt his fist loosen under her hand and flatten against the counter. Watching his expression carefully, the moment his hand slid back far enough for his fingers to make their way in between hers, she pulled away.

"Your to-do list is on the table," she shared, turning her back on him.

~

While Liv was in the back getting ready to go to the shop, Braden sat on the couch looking over the list in his hand without reading it. She touched him. Liv wasn't a toucher. She was more of a smack you on the arm, nudge you with her elbow kind of a girl. Even the night she allowed him to hold her she grabbed his shirt, and never touched him. She was apologizing and he got that, but her touch did more than emphasize how sorry she was for what she said. It made him curious.

Braden stood as soon as Liv stepped back into the living room. Her black hair was completely straight with the sides pinned back away from her face so you could see her black, diamond hoop earrings sway against her jaw. She had on a black t-shirt that read 'BLACK HEART, BLACK SHOES, AND TATTOOS', with black and white plaid slacks. As she continued to the door he followed, noticing the way the plaid pattern stretched wider across her backside and hips as it clung to her, hugging the curve of her thighs.

"Do I got somethin' on me?" she snapped, causing him to look up and see her looking back at him with a slight scowl on her face.

As luck would have it, she did. Braden walked up and peeled a small sticker off of the back of her pants.

Sticking it to the tip of his index finger, he smiled, sharing, "Your ass is 'special'," as he showed her the red and yellow sticker.

With a laugh she assured, "Damn right," before informing, "I made you lunch, it's in the fridge. You'll probably be done before I get back so I'll see you in the morning."

"Cool, thanks."

Liv made a clicking sound with her mouth and winked at him before opening the front door and walking out.

Closing the door behind her, Braden looked at the list still in his hand, but all he could think was, Pat is one lucky bastard and Kieran was a damn fool.

As Braden's mind worked overtime, trying to forget how Liv placing her hand on his made him feel, every other part of him seemed to react to the moment making it hard not to give in to his thoughts of her. It was an unnecessary complication that he neither needed nor wanted. To say, which he had many times, that he never thought of her *that way*, was in fact a lie. The truth was when he did have an inappropriate thought it was quickly replaced by the knowledge of what they meant to each other. Their bond was too pure to be clouded with immorality. Whether it was right or wrong, that's what he had Mina for. Liv was beyond simple thoughts of lust for him. There were boundaries to their relationship, but lately, the foundation of those boundaries had begun to crack and it all started with what he'd read on her kindle.

Spending most of his week tending to Liv's to-do lists, he did everything he could think of to occupy the rest of his time, in an effort to avoid alone time with Mina. That was until her usual pout over not getting her way had turned into a full blown huff causing Braden to give in when she showed up at his apartment Wednesday night with movies in hand suggesting they spend the evening on his couch.

Mina remained snuggled up next to him on the couch while the sappy love story she brought over seemed never ending. In the back of his mind, he couldn't stop himself from tallying the differences between her and Liv. Mina was definitely warm in every sense of the word. Liv on the other hand was the epitome of cool. Mina always came off as subdued, most of the time it was hard for him to tell how she truly felt about something. If Liv had a problem, she let everyone know and if happened to be him that she was mad at, a smack to the back of the head could definitely be expected. Smiling to himself, Braden recalled the time she was so mad at him she wacked him with a broom, repeatedly.

Just as his mind started to wander to the physical differences between the two, Mina broke his train of thought.

"What are you thinking about?"
Braden's smile faded as he glanced at her.

Pushing up at his side, she repeated, "What are you thinking about?"

"Nothin'."
Mina frowned for a second before a cheery smile took over.

"I was thinking, since I met your mom Sunday, it's only fair that you get to meet my parents."

Leaning away from her, he blurted, "How is that fair?"

"You don't want to meet my parents?" She questioned as if she were in shock.

Braden scooted farther away from her, asking, "What makes you think I would want to?"

"We have been dating for almost a year," she snapped at him before instantly calming herself and saying, "It's okay. We can talk about it another time. I know you have a lot on your mind."

He did have a lot on his mind but he would bet his life she had no idea what she was talking about.

Shaking his head at her Braden insisted, "No and I didn't ask you to meet my mom. It happened by accident."

"I know that silly," she replied with a smile before suggesting, "We can wait until you're not so stressed to talk about it."

'Am I not speaking English?' Braden thought to himself, trying to figure out why she was ignoring what he was saying.

"Why would I be stressed?"

Giving him a compassionate pat on the arm, Mina replied, "You got laid-off and now Liv has you running around doing chores for her to make extra money."

"What?"

"Look, it's okay. I've thought about how much she's taking advantage of you and decided to help you out until your back on your feet."

Braden had to close his eyes and pause for a moment before repeating, "What?" instead of shouting, 'Are you crazy' at her.

"I make enough money for both of us."

Shaking his head, trying to make this conversation make sense, Braden informed, "I know I said she hired me but I'm not going to take her money."

"You feel sorry for her but that doesn't mean..."

Agitated, he cut her off informing, "I'm helping her out because I want to. I don't feel sorry for her."

"Come on, you don't have to pretend with me," she assured in a condescending tone.

That's when it hit him. What Liv said about being with Mina seeming forced.

Leaning back, Braden sighed, "I have been pretending."

A soft smile formed on her face as she replied, "Like I said, it's okay."

Although he hated to admit it, the only reason he was into her in the first place was the fact that she was into him.

"It's not and I don't think we should see each other anymore."

Mina's expression went blank and he braced himself for tears and possibly yelling.

The longer Mina sat there quietly staring at him, the more it started to freak him out.

Then suddenly, she snapped, "What is wrong with you?"

Caught off guard he shrugged at her.

Hopping to her feet, she stated, "I'm pretty. I'm sweet. I'm easy going and I come from a good family."

"Okay..." Braden slowly replied, wondering where this was going.

"So what is your problem?" She demanded.

Unsure of what to say, he answered, "I don't know?"

With a light sigh and compassionate eyes, she shared, "I do. You're just confused."

"I am?" He questioned, seeing as at the moment he really was.

"We have been dating for almost a year and now you're out of work. I'm sure that put a hindrance on all your plans for us."

"Plans?"

She may have appeared sweet as pie, but it was growing abundantly clear to him that Mina was crazy as hell as she nodded, saying, "I'll give you some space until you feel like a man again. Then we can get back on track."

At that point, all he wanted was to get her safely out of his apartment. And by safely, he meant his safety.

For some reason, even though she had just declared she was going to give him space, she was still standing in his apartment.

"I'll see you around then." He said, hoping she would get the hint and leave.

"You're breaking up with me?"

Thankful they were now on the same page, Braden replied, "Yeah, I am."

Mina's eyes welled with tears as she questioned, "Why?"

Trying not to get frustrated by the fact that she seemed to be in denial he stood up.

Taking a deep breath, he shared, "Mina, you are very pretty and so sweet," pausing to mentally add passive aggressive and crazy, "But I don't want a relationship. At least not the kind you're looking for."

Pouting, she looked down, complaining, "It's not fair for you to let one girl ruin things for us."

"I'm not. There was never going to be an us."

Mina's eyes grew wide as she looked up at him.

"You're pathetic." She spouted before turning and walking out of his apartment.

Braden sat down on his couch as his door slammed shut.

Sinking down into the couch cushions, he couldn't help thinking she might be right. He was still as empty as he was when he quit playing guitar over two years ago. But there was nothing he wanted. With no desire to love or be loved, he didn't care if he learned or succeeded. Braden wanted almost nothing out of life. Only Thursday night, where beer and pizza with a friend made him feel something, and kept him from completely shutting down.

The first few days of Braden working at the house went well. After hurting his feelings Monday, Liv thought it best to leave as soon as he arrived Tuesday and Wednesday to avoid any awkwardness her apology might bring. It seemed to work. He did exactly what was on his list and was gone before she got home all three days. When Thursday came, she felt sure that everything would be the same as it always was, but when he arrived, an hour early, she knew right away something was wrong.

Tossing the lid on top of the storage bin she was going through, Liv stood up trying to decipher the look on his face as he walked in.

"What's up, you're early?"

Shrugging, Braden replied, "I thought I'd get a head start on my list so everything would be cleaned up before tonight."

"And?" she questioned, waiting for the real reason.

"And what?"

Blowing out a loud breath, she thought, 'fine don't tell me' as she shared, "I'm gonna go get dressed then."

Without saying another word, Braden walked to the kitchen and sat down, looking at his list.

Feeling uneasy, Liv headed to her room. She could feel a change in him and it worried her. She needed Thursdays. She needed him. It was the only time she could let go and feel at peace.

~

Walking back into the living room, a moment of panic and then outrage brought her to a dead stop.

"What the hell?" Liv barked at Braden, seeing him digging through the storage bin she left open.

Seemingly unaware that he was violating her privacy, he smiled up at her, teasing, "I'm trippin' out right now. You write love poems?"

Her anger flared as she marched over to him, assuring, "No."

"You sure?" he laughed before sharing, "'Cause they all say Liv at the bottom. And who is BC?"

Liv's stomach lurched as she lifted the lid and slammed it back onto the bin.

Braden smiled wide at her revealing a folded piece of notebook paper in his hand as he challenged, "Tell me or I'll read it. Looks pretty personal too, with all the hearts."

'I'm gonna kill this punk' flashed in her mind before she lunged to grab it from him.

Holding it just out of reach, he laughed, "You forced my hand."

Just as he opened it, Liv elbowed him in the side causing his arm to drop.

~

As soon as she snatched the letter out of his hand and started to run to her room with it he caught her. The whole love poem thing wasn't really worth an explanation, but his name with hearts all around it was.

"You got a thing for me?"

Liv fought to get away as she growled, "Hell no!"

Struggling to grab the paper from her hand, Braden pulled her against him, pressing her back against his chest as she tried to pull away.

"Damn it! Get off of me!" she shouted.

Without letting go, he laughed, "Let me see it then."

Liv stopped struggling for a moment.

"I used to be into you."

"Sweet, did Kieran know?" he question in a teasing tone.

"It was before I met him."

Loosening his hold on her, he tried to place seeing her anywhere before the night she showed up at a party with Kieran.

"I don't remember you," he admitted as he let go of her.

Crumpling the paper in her fist, she swiped her hair out of her face giving her shoulders a little shake as she turned to face him.

"At a pasture party, you got into my car by accident."

Staring at her, a memory from back then flashed through his mind before he recalled, "You used to have blonde hair..."

"The next day, you were back with Lily and I was over it."

Remorse weighed heavily on Braden as he replied, "Liv..."

Back to her usual self she let out a loud "Ha!" before saying, "It's not a thing. Everybody losses it in one way or another."

It took a minute for him to understand what she meant.

"Liv?"

Walking past him, Liv pressed her finger to his temple, pushing his head back a little, she warned, "Stay outta my stuff, punk."

Watching her as she walked to the other room he recalled a night a few weeks before his high school graduation. He was pissed that Lily had cheated on him again. Getting drunk after playing at a party, he knew he couldn't drive so he'd called Auggie to come get him. Thinking it was the car he drove to the party he climbed in to wait for his brother and ended up on some girl's lap. Most everything was hazy, but he remembered that she felt good. Or more that he felt good. He was drunk and hurt and couldn't have cared less who she was. It was still hands down the best sex he'd ever had. Even though he was drunk and barely remembered her, he remembered that. He'd always assumed it was so hot because it was unexpected. At that time, he'd only been with Lily. As it stood his total was only three with Lily, Mina and a hot blonde in the passenger seat of a car one night. And it turned out it was Liv. Damn...

~

"I'm headin' to the shop." Liv informed before quickly walking to the door and stepping out of the house.

She never would have said anything to him about it and she'd always wondered if he secretly knew. Now that it was out, it was kinda funny to her that he never realized. Then again, he was smashed that night and the next time he saw her, she had jet black hair and was covered in tattoos.

On the way to Legacy Ink, Liv thought about that night.

For two and a half years she'd gone to every party, event and local spot Braden played at just hoping he would notice her. That night when he fell into her lap, literally, she wanted him to never forget her. It was good too. Not as good as it was later on with some experience behind her but since she'd always heard how horrible first times were, it wasn't half bad. Plus, she wasn't too far from being hammered herself.

When Auggie showed up, irritated and honking the horn like the damn jackass that he was, Braden was still kissing her. Something later in life she appreciated about that night. Her experience, with Kieran, was that when a man is done, he doesn't normally linger.

With Auggie out of his truck, cursing and making a scene, Braden gave her one last kiss before asking, "I'll be at the shack tomorrow night, wanna come?"

"I always watch you play," she shared as he flashed a smile at her, the ridiculous one where it was obvious he was biting the side of his tongue, and slid out of the car.

That night taught Liv a lot. So did the next day when she showed up to the shack and his arms were wrapped around Lily's waist. At the time she figured she must not have been worth remembering.

When a week later her grandpa got sick and they moved so her dad could take care of him, Liv decided to reinvent herself. Her first tattoo was so liberating she had to have another and another. Before she knew it both her arms were completely covered. When her grandpa passed and her dad decided to move up north, the once shy girl who left at seventeen came back to town at age twenty-one a completely different person. Tossing around the idea of thanking Braden for that, Liv loved who she became. She never hesitated to speak her mind and damn right she would be heard too. Shyness and fear of how she would be perceived was no longer a part of her. It wasn't an act either. Everything that she became was already in her head all she did was let it out. Giving herself the freedom to be herself was the best thing she'd ever done.

~

Despite what Liv said, Braden couldn't help going back to look through her stuff. It was wrong to invade her privacy and he knew it but he did it anyway. He looked at picture after picture. The ones of him on stage made his stomach hurt. There were notes to friends of hers and from her friends to her that he passed, noticing one said her dream date was to be taken to Fairmont's on the lake. When he came to a spiral buried at the bottom of the box. Flipping through the pages he found more poems she'd written. Stopping at the page that had two separate pictures stuck to it, one of him and one of blonde Liv, his breath grew shallow as he read.

Watching you slide your fingers down the strings

Makes me want for unfamiliar things

Late at night I imagine that it's me

You'd glide you fingers across my skin so effortlessly

♫ ♫ ♫

I see your heart when you're up there

Each note is caressed from out of thin air

♫ ♫ ♫

Commanding the cords obedience as you sing

I can tell something's missing

♫ ♫ ♫

Music isn't what she brings

Her harsh tones control you as she pulls your strings

♫ ♫ ♫

The cord of your heart is what she lacks

If given the chance

I would glide my fingers across your strings

As I played you back.

It was like musician porn. Her words were sexy and each one affected him more as he re-read them.

After pulling out his cell phone and taking a picture of the page, Braden stared at the picture of blonde Liv. There was something in her eyes. The same look Liv always had. Seeing old pictures of her, and knowing her now, it seriously could have been two completely different people, except for her eyes. It was like the Liv he knew was trying to bust out but the shy blonde wouldn't let her. Either way, he knew there was no way he was going to let what happen between them fade into the background of their friendship like she had.

On the way home from Legacy Ink, while 'Gives You Hell' by All-American Rejects blared through her car speakers, Liv reassured herself that nothing was different. She could easily say Braden had backed her into a corner and she was forced to tell him. That was almost true. Except, she wasn't backed into a corner, she was pressed up against his chest with his arms around her. When her mind shifted to what it would feel like to have him back her into a corner, Liv cursed herself under her breath.

It was odd that they had become friends in the first place. When someone breaks your heart, it teaches you a lesson. Seeing that person again and realizing they've learned nothing from it, pisses you off. But when you're forced to sit by and watch someone unwind with heartache as the whole world watches, that's the moment you realize you're thankful for the lesson they taught you and that person deserves a chance. And that's what she gave him, a chance to start over with her. Now, she couldn't imagine what would have happened to either of them at this point, had they not had each other. That was what she needed to focus on. Not a moment from the past but right now. It was Thursday night, and that is what needed to be preserved, for both their sakes.

~

Seated at the kitchen table, playing round three of chutes and ladders, conversation was nonexistent. The sound of their game pieces sliding across the board with each turn was starting to make Liv uncomfortable. Although the silence that accompanied Braden was usually comforting, she could feel the unspoken strain her admission this morning placed on the evening.

Glancing at him as she made the final move to win, Liv said, "Three outta three."

Without a word, he stood up and walked to the kitchen sink.

Twisting in her chair, she looked past the bar to him, offering, "If you've got somethin' to say, say it."

Braden turned around and walked to his side of the bar, asking, "Why didn't you want me to know?"

"For all I knew you did." Liv shot back at him, in an irritated tone.

Appearing confused, he questioned, "How?"

"You were there," she replied with a laugh.

He stared at her for a moment before looking down at the bar.

"Don't you think I would have said somethin'?"

"And what would you have said?" she questioned with a smirk, thinking 'this should be good'.

Wrinkling his brow in thought, it appeared he didn't have an answer.

Liv could have let it go seeing as she made her point but instead, she hopped out of the chair and stepped to her side of the bar.

"Who would you have said somethin' to? Me or Kieran?" she asked, taunting, "Four years later when Kieran introduced us at Pat's party? Would you have pulled me to the side? Or would you have caught up with him later?"

"I don't know."

Scoffing at his answer, she assured, "It doesn't matter anyway. It was a long time ago and like I said, it's not a thing."

Braden lowered his voice almost to a whisper, reminding, "You were a virgin."

The way he said 'virgin' made her laugh as she realized why he felt bad.

Relieved it was guilt that he was struggling with, Liv shared, "Give that conscience of yours a break. You can't steal something that's willingly given," then winked at him, and headed to her room.

~

Stretched out on Liv's couch, Braden couldn't get himself back into the right frame of mind.

There was some guilt in knowing he was her first and how it played out, but all he could think about was the smell of whiskey in a car, and kisses that turned needy along with heavy breath. Frustrated from his thoughts, there was nothing he could do about the growing tension as he lay there.

Trying to get comfortable even though he knew it was going to be impossible at this point, Braden rolled on his side. Staring across the living room, he could faintly see down the hallway to Liv's bedroom door. Focusing on it, he wondered what she was doing in there. Was she laying there thinking about that night too? Maybe she was reading. What if she was, and it was a book like he saw on her kindle. If it was, how wrong would it be if he went in there and offered her a helping hand? That's what friends do right, they help each other?

Braden sat up. Continuing to stare down the hallway, he thought about how close he was to Liv. Every Thursday he spent the night on her couch. After drinking and playing games at her table, pretending her body was the furthest thing from his mind. As he stood up, he thought about a girl he didn't know and how she eased his pain. He took one step forward. One step before thoughts of the woman he knew and how broken she was when he held her, caused him to sit back down.

The little bell over the door rang as Liv entered Legacy Ink. She wasn't two steps in when her cell phone buzzed in her hand.

B: I think you forgot something.

Drawing in a deep breath, she ignored the text and continued into the shop.

"Rough morning?" Jimmy laughed from behind the counter as Liv gave him the finger and continued to the back.

Throwing her purse on the chair, Liv noticed Penny was right behind her.

Pursing her lips up into a smile, Penny asked, "So...today is pajama day?"

"Sexy, right?" she sarcastically replied, pulling a black elastic band from around her wrist.

"Are you alright?"

Nodding, Liv replied, "Without a doubt, beautiful."

Penny scowled a bit then gave a weak smile as she walked out of the room.

Pulling her hair up into a ponytail before looping it around to make a loose bun, Liv continued to ignore the buzzing of her phone. She dug through the desk drawers until she found a black and white patterned handkerchief. Folding it, she made herself a wide headband that covered the top of her barely brushed hair. As she stepped over to the mirror she grabbed her lipstick out of her purse, thankful she at least had the sense to put her chuck's on before she left the house.

Everything was thrown off kilter from the moment she woke up late. She didn't hear her alarm, then when she did get up, Braden was already awake. That would have been fine though, except the burner on her gas stove went out and she couldn't get it to re-light. When Braden tried, he got it but because it was turned on high for the fifteen minutes while she was trying, a huge flame shot up and scared the hell out of both of them. He dropped the lighter onto the burner and it burst before either one of them could turn the burner off. By the time the catastrophe was over, Liv lost two cup towels, her favorite pan, and her whole house smelled like gas and burnt plastic. As insane as her stove catching on fire was, that wasn't what sent her out of the house in a black tank top and skull and crossbones pajama bottoms. It was when she was trying to air out the house and Braden came up beside her to help her open one of the windows that wouldn't budge. Pushing up from both sides, when it broke free and opened, it happened so fast, she lost her balance and almost fell. Braden caught her before she hit the floor, and she appreciated that, but when she was steady and his hand on her side tightened at her waist, she couldn't get out of there fast enough.

After smoothing her lipstick over her lips, Liv looked at herself in the mirror. Her view was darkened slightly by the aviator sunglasses she planned to wear all day in the absence of eye makeup. Making a face in the mirror, she mentally chastised herself for not being able to shake off the urges Braden's touch invoked.

~

Straight from the shop to The Dog House after work, Liv sat on a barstool at the far corner of the bar. Texting Charlotte, she waited for Auggie to make his way over.

"Nice pj's." Auggie teased.

Laughing, Liv replied, "Gin and tonic."

"Bad day?" he questioned, walking to the center of the bar to make her drink.

As he set her glass down in front of her, Liv shared, "Your brother damn near caught my whole kitchen on fire this morning."

"So you said screw it I'm not getting dressed today?"

She smirked at him, answering, "Somethin' like that."

Auggie laughed, offering, "I know you got sleeves but you need a jacket. It's supposed to be in the fifties tonight."

Lifting her drink, she assured, "This should keep me warm," before taking a sip and then drinking the rest down. "Another."

"You okay?" he questioned with a scowl on his face.

"You bet."

Auggie gave a slight grunt in disbelief as he turned to make her another drink.

Once drink number two was out of the way, Liv took her time slowly sipping her third gin and tonic. She wanted to relax and clear her mind, not get sloppy fall off the barstool drunk. As the bar started to fill up with the usual Friday night crowd, she glanced down at her phone.

C: If you keep turning him down, he's going to stop asking.

L: It hasn't stopped him yet.

C: What's stopping you?

L: It's complicated.

C: Call it what you like. I still say go for it.

~

Walking into the back door of The Dog House, Braden walked straight into Charlotte's office instead of heading to the main area of the bar.

"Got a minute?" he asked, pulling her attention away from her cell phone as she looked up at him.

Charlotte quickly sent a text then set her phone down saying, "What's up?"

"Who was that?" he questioned, eyeing her phone on the desk.

Curling the corner of her mouth into a smile, she flipped her cell face down as she replied, "Did you need something?"

Closing her office door, he asked, "Can you keep a secret?"

Eyeing him suspiciously, she replied, "Yes."

Braden took a deep breath before confessing, "I'm kinda diggin' Liv."

Charlotte appeared more confused and less surprised then he thought she should.

"Oh-kay..."

Giving her a dirty look, Braden griped, "Just okay, that's it?"

Shrugging a shoulder at him, she added, "I'm sure you are."

"Am I missing something?"

Charlotte looked like she was about to laugh as she questioned, "Were you expecting it to be a big deal?"

"Yeah!" he blurted, wondering why it wasn't.

Appearing as though she felt bad for letting him down, she replied, "Sorry, I didn't know this was some sort of a revelation for you."

Baffled, he couldn't help standing there shaking his head at her.

Standing up from behind her desk, Charlotte walked over to him.

Holding her hands up, she shared, "Look, I don't judge."

"What's that supposed to mean?"

With a hint of knowing in her expression she shared, "I just assumed since y'all hook up once a week..."

Taken aback he cut her off, swearing, "No, we don't."

"Then what do the two of you do every Thursday night?" Charlotte questioned with an air of disbelief.

"Drink beer and play board games."

"Seriously?"

Nodding, Braden asked, "What would make you think that?"

Laughing at him, she replied, "Don't sound so offended."

"I'm not, but we're not and why would you think we were?"

As her laughter faded she answered, "It seemed reasonable seeing as you won't commit to Mina and she's holding back from getting with Pat."

Braden paused to think for a moment before asking, "Holding back as in..." leaving the question open for her to fill in the blank.
Charlotte quickly turned and walked behind her desk.

Taking a seat, she smiled, replying, "You should break up with Mina and ask her out."

"I did," he shared before clarifying, "Break up with Mina."

"Then I suggest you get to her before Pat does."

It took a minute of her glancing between him and the door with a serious expression before he got the hint and walked out.

Scanning the crowd, Braden looked for Liv on his way up to the bar. Spotting her sitting alone was a relief. He stayed focused on her, watching her red lips sip from the drink in her hand, leaving their mark against the glass as he made his way over. When he reached her, Braden stood at her side instead of taking a seat. As she stared down into her glass, he stole it from her grasp and took a sip.

"Gin?"

Keeping her eyes down, Liv replied, "Tastes like it."

Braden glanced over seeing his brother with a hard scowl across his face hold up four fingers.

"You wanna get a table?" he cautiously asked, knowing she only drank liquor when she was upset.

Lowering her forehead to the palms of her hands, she shook her head.

"Take me home."

~

The drive out to the farmhouse was silent. It wasn't until they were inside that Liv said a word to him.

Opening her refrigerator, she offered, "Beer?" Braden wished she would take her sunglasses off, as she handed him a bottle. He could see her eyes but just barely and not enough to figure out what was wrong.

Setting his beer on the counter, he watched her grab one for herself, saying, "You can go."

"I don't want to."

Shaking her head, she urged, "Please. Go."

Reaching to her face, Braden pulled her sunglasses off before asking, "Why?"

"I want to be alone."

Finding it hard to believe her, he questioned, "Then why were you at the bar?"

"I wanted to drink."

Frustration started to build inside him at the thought of her not wanting him there.

"And what? Pat not showing up just ruined your night?"

"I don't have to explain myself to you."

Liv was right, she didn't but that didn't stop him from wanting her to.

"I would never turn you away." Braden swore as he walked passed her.

It took several attempts of turning the key in the ignition, and jiggling wires under the hood before Braden caved and called his brother. He hated asking Auggie for help but had no choice when his El Camino wouldn't start. While he waited, Penny and Seth showed up, which was cool because he liked hanging with Seth but then Mina walked over at the exact same time Auggie drove up in his diesel with both Charlotte and Liv.

As the three of them hopped out of Auggie's truck, Charlotte and Liv were laughing which happened to piss Braden off a little.

"Don't ya think it's about time to let the old girl die a peaceful death?"

Penny instantly joined Auggie, teasing, "Oh please, you know that's his baby."

"Isn't it a classic?"

Braden gave Seth a quick nod of appreciation as he replied, "Yeah, she is."

He had almost forgotten Mina was there until she stepped forward, asking, "Is your car broken?"

Before Braden had the chance to answer, Liv opened his car door, saying, "She's in need of good jump," as she slid into the driver's side.

"He called the right man then." Charlotte insinuated with a sly smile.

Liv slid out of the car and stood up holding her sunglasses that Braden had walked out of her house with the night before.

Braden fussed, "Don't talk dirty about my girl."

Penny laughed, "See."

Sliding her sunglasses on, Liv smirked, "You left your lights on, punk."

Sure enough, when he looked at the steering column, she was right. Damn it.

It took a minute for everyone's teasing to subside. After all the jokes were out of the way, Auggie jumped Braden's car and it started right away.

As they stood in the parking lot while Braden let his car run to recharge the battery, Penny asked, "So what's everyone doing today?"

Charlotte answered, "We're taking Liv to get her car from The Dog House then she and I are going shopping. You want to come?"

"Mina and I are going to lunch."

Charlotte gave Braden an odd look that he mirrored in return.

"I though you two broke up?" she questioned directly at Mina.

Penny quickly looked at Mina asking, "Y'all broke up?"

Before she could reply, Liv glared at Braden, "You broke up with her?"

"We broke up."

"He broke up with me." Mina pouted in a soft voice right before Braden griped, "I broke up with her. Damn."

Braden stood there wondering if there was any way for the situation to be more awkward. Maybe his mom could stop by and then they could invite Pat over.

Everyone was silent until Auggie walked over and closed Braden's hood.

"Game's on. You got beer?"

Braden gave his brother an 'of course I do' nod before asking, "Seth, you stayin'?"

"Sure." Seth replied before Penny cautioned, "Only one beer, okay."

As they all stared at her in horror, Penny defended herself, saying, "What? It lower's sperm count."

Auggie, griped, "Oh, what the hell," and turned, walking towards Braden's apartment.

Shaking his head at his sister, Braden urged Seth to follow, saying, "Come on, man," as he took off to his apartment also.

"I'm serious," Penny swore as Seth followed him.

With a wide smile, Braden assured, "Gotcha, Pen, only one beer."

~

The second the guys were inside Braden's apartment, Liv noticed an interested look on Penny's face as she turned to Mina.

"When did y'all break up?"

A pitiful expression coated Mina's face as she re-emphasized who was responsible, "He broke up with me Wednesday night."

Liv was glad Braden broke it off with her before he found out about their high school hook up. That meant she was guilt free in the break up and actually kinda proud of him for finally cutting her loose.

"Well, are ya grievin' or grateful?"

Mina gave Liv a confused look, questioning, "Am I what?"

With a slight huff, Charlotte explained, "Is this the first day you've drug yourself out of bed or are you like 'woo, I dodged that bullet'."

When Mina still appeared confused, Penny asked, "Are you happy or sad?"

Liv and Charlotte looked at each other as Mina gave a heavy sigh, replying, "Sad."

Giving a sigh of her own, Liv offered, "Come on then."

"Penny and I are supposed to go to lunch."

"And now y'all are shopping with us," Liv informed, opening the door to Auggie's truck.

Mina managed to get out a, "But..." before Charlotte cut her off, saying, "No buts. Just get in."

~

Although Liv felt a certain satisfaction in how uncomfortable Mina appeared while shopping, she wasn't sure why she was acting that way. They had never been anything but nice to her. If Liv had to guess, Mina had a plan to get Braden back through Penny and she just ruined her day. Why else would she have asked Penny to lunch without telling her they broke up?

Sitting at Lostracca's waiting for their food to arrive, the table was fairly silent, giving Liv an opportunity to get down to the bottom of Mina's intentions.

"So, Miss Mina, why did y'all break up?"

The look on her face leaned toward her saying, 'that's private' as she replied, "I'm not sure why he broke up with me."

Unable to help the nerve it struck each time Mina reminded them, it was Braden that did the breaking up and she was just an innocent victim, Liv rolled her eyes.

"What?"

Visibly trying not to laugh, Charlotte replied, "We get it."

Mina frowned, looking down at the table as Penny questioned, "He really just broke up with you out of nowhere?"

Turning to Penny as if she was her oldest friend in the world, Mina answered, "Everything was perfectly fine. All our plans were right on schedule until he got laid-off."

Penny gave her a strange look, much like the one Charlotte and Liv were giving her, as she asked, "My brother was making plans?"

Shrugging slightly, Mina informed, "Until he got preoccupied," shifting her eyes from Penny to Liv.

"What? With me?" Liv blurted across the table.

Mina's expression leaned toward a dirty look until her pitiful one took back over as she softly replied, "We were supposed to spend every day together, then you decided to need him every day."

Penny's eyes went wide as she covered her mouth with her hand leaning towards Charlotte, who clearly wasn't sure whether to laugh or not.

'Alright' Liv thought as she glared at Mina.

"Well, he didn't have to say yes."

With a snort Mina fussed, "Like he was going to say no to you."

"I don't know what you think..." Liv started before Mina cut her off, saying, "Yes you do. You know he feels sorry for you and you take advantage of it."

Liv took a sip of her drink and cleared her throat before imparting, "Now I see why he broke up with you. Braden has a lot of faults and no doubt our friendship is one of them, but if there's one thing he took away from his relationship with Lily, it's how to spot manipulative bullshit from a mile away. So if you really think I'm the reason, I feel sorry for you," putting Mina right in her place and an end to the conversation.

The game had been over for a while when Charlotte and Penny got back to Braden's apartment.

As soon as they walked in, Penny questioned, "Why is Seth in the corner?"

Auggie laughed with Braden as they looked over at Seth sitting on a stool in the corner.

"He was cheering for the wrong team." Auggie shared before Penny snapped, "So you put him in the corner?"

"Why are you there, Seth?"

Seth stood, saying, "Because that's how you learn."

Shaking her head with a laugh, Charlotte sat down on Auggie's lap watching Penny's face turn red.

"Are you drunk?"

Seth shook his head at her.

"Have you been drinking?"

A wide smile formed on Seth's face as he nodded.

Glaring at Braden, she griped, "Didn't I say one beer?"

"I had...no beers." Seth chuckled as Braden assured, "He really didn't."

"We gave him whiskey instead." Auggie informed with a nod.

"Ugh." Penny exhaled as Seth stepped to her. Wrapping his arms around her, he kissed her cheek then whispered in her ear.

Penny's disposition instantly changed as she let out a giggle before saying, "Bye," and practically dragging Seth out of the apartment.

Not long after Penny and Seth left, Charlotte and Auggie also left, leaving Braden alone in his apartment. As he sat there, staring at his T.V. without watching what was on, his cell phone pinged.

L: You busy?
Braden shook his head, still angry with her as he texted back.

B: No. Maybe I want to be alone.

L: Don't be a girl, punk.

B: Glad you're all better now.

L: WTF?

B: See you in the morning.
When she didn't respond, he tossed his cell on the couch cushion beside him and walked to his bedroom.

~

Instead of getting out of her car and going into her house, Liv put her car in reverse and backed out of her driveway.

Tapping on Braden's door, Liv waited for him to answer.

The door cracked open but only a few inches as he questioned, "What?"

"You busy?"

"What do you want?"

Fighting the urge to snap at him, Liv asked, "Can I come in?"

Opening the door a little more Braden repeated, "What do you want?"

"I didn't turn you away. I wanted to be alone."

Flashing a sarcastic smile, Braden said, "Oh, well I'm not telling you you can't come in," then shut the door in her face.

Blowing out a loud breath, she thought, 'gah, he's such a girl sometimes'.

Staring at his door, Liv asked herself why she was there. Why did she even care if he was mad at her? All of this was his fault anyway. He was the reason she bailed from her house in only her pajamas yesterday. The reason she told Pat no, for the twentieth time. He was who she was trying to drink off her mind, and why she wanted to be alone last night.

She could feel the buildup. It had been happening for some time now. There was hope that it wouldn't but deep down Liv knew it would eventually. Seeing him every day just happened to usher in the inevitable along a bit quicker. It didn't matter if she could blame him or not, everything changes.

As she thought about kicking his door before turning and walking away, it opened.

"You wanna ride with me to get somethin' to eat?"

Nodding, she stepped into his apartment.

"You need to learn how to pick up after yourself." Liv teased as she walked into his living room.

"Feel free to start tidying up if it bothers you."

Shooting him a dirty look, she snapped, "I get that you're mad, okay."

Mad seem like an understatement as Braden turned and looked down at her.

"You do? You get that I'm mad?"

Taking a step back, she assured, "Don't get loud with me, punk."

He took a step towards her.

"Don't get loud with you?"

Giving him a little shove, Liv spouted, "Do you have anything real to say or are you just going to keep repeating me?"

"You want me to say something real?"

Liv couldn't help finding humor in how absurd their argument was.

She was starting to wonder if he even knew why he was mad at her or if he just felt he should be because she asked him to leave. Before she could say anything her cell vibrated in her pocket loud enough for both of them to hear.

"Is that Pat?" Braden griped at her.

"How the hell am I supposed to know?" Liv replied before taunting, "I'm starting to think you have a thing for him."

Narrowing his eyes at her, he questioned, "You don't even care what kind of a person he is, do you?"

"No, I really don't," she snapped back, frustrated and honestly done with the argument.

"You'll just give it up to anybody then?"

Insulted she looked him up and down, spouting, "Clearly."

"So this is you punishing me for something I didn't know until a few days ago?"

"I'm not punishing you for anything."

"But you'll go to someone like him for that when I'm right here."

Almost choking on her words, Liv spit out, "Wait! What?"

The air between them felt thin as his statement soaked in. It didn't matter that he was the one who said it, Braden seemed just as caught off guard as she was.

Nervous curiosity swelled inside her as she stood there waiting to see what would happen next. Was he going to apologize? Would he be a man about it and make a move? Or was he just going to stand there and stare at her?

When it was obvious he had nothing else to say, Liv swallowed hard and said, "I'm gonna go."

"Okay."

"See you in the morning?" she questioned, turning to open the door.

"Okay."

Walking out of Braden's apartment, Liv thought 'what the hell just happened' before accepting a comforting, yet disappointing, realization. Nothing. Nothing happened.

On the way out to Liv's, Braden thought of different ways to ask her out. That's what Charlotte had advised in the first place and definitely what he should have done instead of suggesting she have meaningless sex with him. Not that it would be meaningful, but it could be. Maybe. That was beside the point. He knew how he felt about her, but had no idea what that meant if they started dating or went on a date. Just one date, he reminded himself, to stop getting carried away. Damn, if he didn't get a handle on himself, there's no telling what would come out of his mouth this time.

Pulling the extra key out of the cement boots by the door when she didn't answer, Braden concentrated on what he was going to say while forcing back the look she had on her face when he all but propositioned her. At first he thought 'she's going to knock my ass out' then as he watched her expression, she seemed...interested, hopeful, ready to get naked? But instead of giving her look the attention it deserved, he stood there saying 'okay' like a frickin' dumbass.

Liv wasn't in the living room, giving him one last chance to psych himself up and ask her out.

With a deep breath, he called her name thinking, it couldn't go any worse than yesterday.

~

"Hey!" Liv heard Braden holler, instantly sending a nervous feeling into the pit of her stomach.

"In my room!"

Instead of waiting in the kitchen like she thought he would, his voice was right outside her door.

"You wanna go out?"

Freezing in place, she questioned, "Like to the bar?"

"No, on a date."

Stepping closer to her door, she asked, "Why?"

It took him a minute to reply, "Why not?"

"Where?"

"We could go to Fairmont's on the lake."

Blinded by outrage, Liv disregarded the fact that she was only wearing a white wife-beater undershirt, red and white boy cut underwear with red and white tube socks as she flung her door open.

He immediately started backing up as she questioned, "Why would you suggest Fairmont's?"

Braden's expression as he retreated to the living room was all the confirmation she needed.

Making her way over, she shoved her finger in his face and fussed, "You went through my stuff."

"Yeah, I did."

"Didn't I tell you not to?" she asked, planting her palms firmly against his chest before shoving him back.

Falling back onto the couch, he looked up at Liv, saying, "I wanted to know more about the girl that was crushing on me, coming to every party just because I was there. The girl that gave it up to me without a second thought, the one that wrote poems and love songs about me."

Glancing up at the ceiling to take a deep breath, she blew it out as she looked down at him, assuring, "That girl's long gone just like the boy she thought she was in love with."

"I want the woman that's standing in front of me."

Shocked at how upfront he was being, Liv blurted, "Ha! You want me?"
Braden's expression grew serious as he nodded at her.

Liv's anger over his violation of her privacy turned into a curious need to see how far he was willing to take this. After all, he went from lets go to dinner to I want you far too quickly, causing her to wonder if he even meant what he was saying.

Stepping between his legs, she pressed her hands against him, pushing his shoulders back and leaning over him questioning, "Why do you want me?"

Inches from her face, he whispered, "I don't know."

His answer was just as disappointing as the fact that his hands were holding on to the sides of his own shorts and he wasn't even trying to touch her.

Aching to prove a point with him, she held onto his shoulders and slid onto his lap. Her knees forced his hands away from his shorts but instead of resting them on her thighs, he pressed his palms into the couch cushions.

"You do want me." Liv confirmed with a smirk, feeling him beneath her before saying, "But 'I don't know' isn't an answer."

His entire body tensed as he leaned his head back against the wall.

Grabbing the front of his shirt pressing herself completely against him, she demanded, "Answer me."

Braden opened his mouth as if to answer but a ragged breath was all that came out.

"You're not man enough for me." Liv announced as she pushed away from him and hopped back on her feet.

Turning towards her bedroom, she slowly walked away from him, mentally claiming victory over the moment.

Closing her bedroom door behind herself she thought, 'If I had kissed him, he probably would have lost it in his pants'. Poor Braden, his relationship with Lily had stunted him. She'd messed with his mind for so many years he had no idea how to handle a real woman. Which was understandable but if he was going to come at her like he did, flat out saying that he wanted her, then he need to come at her like a man. Sadly, between both Lily and Mina, the only thing he knew was how to be was manipulated.

Throwing herself back onto her bed, she let her legs hang over the end so the toes of her socks could brush against the carpet. Climbing onto Braden's lap wasn't the best direction she could have taken with him. Now she had worked herself up along with him and was left with a cautious 'I don't know' in the other room instead of a man in her bed.

She didn't answer the knock at her bedroom door, but it opened anyway. Without feeling the need to get up, she turned her head towards Braden as he walked into her room.

~

"How was I supposed to answer something like that?" he asked, trying to make sense of what just happened.
Braden watched the bed shake as she laughed her reply.
"With honesty."

Confused, he questioned, "Are you screwing with me?"

"You could have said anything."

"I did say something."

"No, you didn't. You said I don't know and that's a damn lie."

"How is it a lie?"

"Because it isn't the truth. The truth would have been if you'd said, knowing we already did it once is messing with me, or you mean something to me, or even saying I need to get off and you're the only one here."

Looking her over, he asked, "Am I something to you?"

Tilting her head away from him, Liv focused on the ceiling as she answered, "You're a lot of things to me."

"Like what?"

"Friend, reason, virginity thief..." she replied, trailing off the moment. Braden leaned over her, bracing himself with his hands against the bed at her sides.

"You can't steal something that's willingly given to you."

Biting her bottom lip, Liv looked up at him, asking, "So why do you want me?"

Without a second thought he swore, "Because you're an incredible, badass woman, who's rockin' the sexiest red and white socks I've ever seen."

Wrapping her hands around his wrists, Liv pushed herself up, so she was sitting in front of him.

Her lips were less than an inch from his mouth as she informed, "You have ten minutes before I have to shower and head to the shop."

Taking her ultimatum seriously, Braden pushed her back on the bed, grabbed the sides of her underwear and yanked them off before he grabbed hold of her arms and jerked her off of the bed. Swinging her around, he pulled Liv against him. He wanted to take her slow but the moment he kissed her, her hands were inside his shorts.

His memory of that night in high school may have been hazy but his body sure as hell remembered her and it was all he could do to hold on as he lifted her off of her feet and took her up against her bedroom door.

'Holy hell,' Liv thought as she stepped into the shower. With basically no foreplay he had her there in less than five minutes. Her skin tingled at the thought and her thighs still felt like they were on fire. Leaning her back against the cool tiles of the shower wall, she still hadn't caught her breath. Braden was fierce, greedy and needy all at the same time. And the way he continued to kiss her after without pulling away. Shaking her head at herself as she stepped under the water, she had to laugh. She might have to come up with a new nickname for him. He was a lot of things, but definitely not a punk.

Dressed and ready to head out, she stepped into her room to see if Braden was still where she'd left him. He had taken the liberty of sitting on the end of her bed while she was in the shower.

"I didn't expect it to be so...rushed."

Liv looked over at him, sharing, "I didn't think you had it in you."

"Maybe you brought it out of me."

Giving him a wink, she turned to leave the room.

Leaning back into the doorway, Liv snapped her fingers and pointed at Braden as she blurted, "Thanks for the hot sex."

As he flashed a wide smile at her, she almost stepped back into the room and kissed him.

~

Sitting on the end of Liv's bed, Braden had gone over what happened so many times now in his mind. While she slid away as he was kissing her, watching her walk into the bathroom, when she was in the shower, as she left for the shop, and still he had no idea how it happened. He had a purpose. To ask her out and see how everything played out from there. He knew himself well. Sure he was impulsive, but in the fun let's go skinny dipping or shoot to the next town and get a burger at four in the morning way. Not have furious unprotected sex with his cousin's widow up against the door like a frickin' mad man, impulsive.

Trying to be rational, he thought on the one hand the way he acted with her was not how he normally treated a woman. Then, on the other hand, she told him he wasn't man enough for her and something deep inside him needed to prove her wrong. Either way, there was no coming back from what they'd done. Not for him.

~

Snapping her fingers as she paced back and forth in front of Kieran's grave, Liv worked up the courage to tell him what she'd done.

Everything was great, bordering on perfect when 'Got You' from The Flys came on the radio. The memory of Auggie laughing saying he didn't think Kieran had a chance in hell but Kieran kept saying, 'nah, I got her just where I want her' flickered through her mind. Then guilt swelled in her chest until she turned off at the intersection and headed to the cemetery, instead of Legacy Ink.

Finally, she blew out a loud breath and blurted, "I got down with Braden this morning." Half expecting more than silence she taunted him.

"It was good and I'll probably let him do me again. If you don't like it you can come back and haunt me or whatever."

When he didn't rise up out of the grave and say something to her, Liv admitted, "I know you're not here."

Staring at his gravestone, she fussed, "If you hadn't been an asshole and died on me, it never would have happened."

Liv let out a loud sigh as she shared, "I'm not mad at you anymore. That's not what this is about. I don't know what I would have done if he hadn't been here when you left me."

Taking a deep breath she finished by saying, "I know what you're thinking and you're wrong. This happened because I wanted it to. Not because of a stupid tattoo. I'm not going to forget about you. I swear. It's just...sex. You can understand that, right?"

Nodding at Kieran's silent grave Liv turned to walk back to her car.

~

Catching himself humming when he stepped out of the shower and again while brushing his teeth, Braden couldn't help but smile. It was rare that things turned out as good as they were in his head. Although he never let his thoughts of Liv go as far as they went today, the realness in the way her kiss tasted against his mouth and how her body felt moving with his was better than anything he could have imagined.

Braden stretched out on his bed. Debating on whether to call her, his phone rang.

"What's up, Pen-Pen?"

His sister's voice sounded concerned as she asked, "Have you talked to Liv today?"

"I was there this mornin', why?"

"I don't know she seemed, off today."

Feeling a concern of his own grow, he questioned, "Off how?"

"Like she couldn't concentrate, I guess."

He couldn't help smile as he shared, "She was good when she left the house."

There was a long pause before Penny said, "You know Kieran's birthday is next week."

"Yeah..." Braden acknowledged, feeling his smile fade.

"Do you remember last year? She took a baseball bat to their porch swing and then set it on fire in the front yard."

He hated being reminded that Liv missed his cousin's sorry ass.

"So?"

"So... I was thinking we could all go out of town, the six of us. Just for a few days and maybe it won't be so hard on her. Uncle Brennen has that cabin that no one ever uses."

Braden wasn't mad at his sister, but his irritation over the subject started to grow anyway.

"Has she said anything about his birthday?"

Sounding confused, Penny replied, "Well no, but..."

"Then why do you want to bring it up. Maybe she's over him."

"Braden!"

"Because he was such a great husband, that's not possible?"

Penny's tone was short as she fussed, "What is your problem?"

Taking a deep breath, Braden reminded himself that to keep Liv from the added pain of finding out Kieran was a cheating bastard when he died, they agreed not to tell Penny or Charlotte either.

"Look, Pen, all I'm sayin' is eventually it's going to be just another day for her and the sooner everyone stops making it an event, the easier it will be on her."

"Okay, geez. Sorry for askin'," she griped before hanging up on him.

~

Rolling over in bed, Liv blinked a few times before picking up her cell phone that was vibrating against the top of the night stand. She rubbed her eyes, trying to focus on the text message that woke her.

B: You up?

L: No

B: You're not?

L: I'm asleep.

B: See you in the morning.

L: Sure thing.

B: 'Night.

L: 'Night.

A light smile formed as Liv shook her head into her pillow before drifting back to sleep.

Seated on a barstool in her kitchen, Liv poured herself a bowl of cereal as her front door swung open. Repressing a smile, her back straightened and her shoulders tensed. Focusing on eating her cereal, she knew he was in a good mood without having to look at him. It was the way his shoes sounded against her hardwood floor. They made a clomping sound, almost like he was stomping. When he was upset, it was always a slow heel to toe step that created a dragging swoosh.

The closer his footsteps became, the more she could feel the tiny prickles of anticipation on the surface of her skin intensify.

Stopping at the opposite side of the bar, Braden leaned forward resting his elbows against it, greeting, "'Morning."

Without a reply, she slid a box of fruit loops over to him.

"Cereal?"

Fighting the smile that was trying to come through her tone, Liv replied, "I didn't make it to the grocery store."

"You want me to go for you?"

Shaking her head she took a bite of her cereal.

After three bites, the silence was more than Liv could take and she looked up to see why he was being so quiet.

"Why are you looking at me like that?" she questioned, realizing he had probably been smiling at her since he walked in.

"So, Fairmont's?"

"No."

"No?"

"That's what I said."

Braden's smile remained fixed as he asked, "Why not?"

"Because I'm not going on a date with you," she assured with a stern expression.

His smile grew wider as he questioned, "Did you sleep good last night?"

A smile of her own broke free before she reigned it in and took another bite of her cereal.

"Yesterday morning..." he started before she promptly cut him off, informing, "Was a one time thing."

Braden's smile faded for a moment before spreading across his face again as he questioned, "Really?"

Doing her best to brush him off, so they could get back to normal, Liv shared, "Look, the sex was hot but I'm just not into you like that."

Appearing as though he wanted to laugh, Braden cleared his throat and nodded.

What Liv imagined would be a feeling of relief turned into regret, then interest as he walked around to her side of the bar.

"What?"

Leaning as close as possible, without touching her, he questioned, "You're not into me?"

Blowing out a short breath, she insisted, "No."

Another nod preceded his, "Okay."

Liv's breathing picked up as he stepped behind her.

She started to question him, but stopped as he brushed her hair back from the side of her face and whispered, "Yes, you are," in her ear.

Slowly shaking her head, she felt his hands slide around her waist then down the front of her thighs while his lips grazed her earlobe.

"Eat your cereal then," he dared, challenging her like she had done with him the previous morning.

Fighting to keep her composure, she focused on the spoon that she couldn't seem to get a grip on.

The tiny prickles resting on the surface seeped through her skin down into her bones, chipping away at her resolve as Braden pressed his hands against the tops of her thighs. Kneading his way back to her waist with one hand. When his other slipped into the front of her pajama bottoms, Liv surrendered. Leaning her head back, she let out a soft moan that was instantly stifled by his kiss.

"You taste like fruit loops." He smiled against her mouth.

An involuntary groan prevented her from smiling back as the sensation his fingers coaxed caused her to shudder from the inside out.

Reaching back, Liv grabbed the shoulders of his t-shirt, twisting them in her hands as she murmured, "Braden..."

~

A rush of animalistic pride coursed through Braden's veins the moment his name came out of her mouth. His vision blurred and it was possible he blacked out momentarily. Furiously pulling her off of the barstool, he did everything in his power to provoke his name from her lips, again.

When the sweet sound of Liv calling his name echoed in his ears for a second time, Braden's entire body shook as he growled her name in return. Holding himself over her, her back was flat against the table top and her pajama bottoms were still hanging off one of her legs that were wrapped around his waist. He gazed down watching her breathe. With each deep breath, he noticed she wasn't trying to catch her breath. It was as if she was breathing for the first time. Savoring the air around her, around them. As he pulled her against his chest and kissed her, in his mind, he could still see her laying there basking in glorious satisfaction. It was a sight Braden knew he would never forget.

'Damn, I meant to go slow this time,' Braden reminded himself as he sat at the table while Liv was in the shower. It was insane that this was the second time, historically the third, and he was yet to see her naked. What was even crazier was how quickly he lost control with her. It was as if once her body peaked, it then demanded that he follow. He was, by nature, a slow and steady type of guy but this...this thing between them, was throwing him off balance. Sex was different with Liv. One minute he was completely in control of himself then in the next, his brain was on fire. He had always considered himself passionate, in a gentle sort of way. The idea of softly making love to a woman had always warmed his blood but being close to Liv scalded him, burning away every sane thought he had. Before today, he never needed to hear a woman moan his name, he didn't want to own her either, but thirty minutes ago, when both actually happened, he growled his victory.

~

Standing in her room just inside the door, Liv tried to wrap her mind around what Braden did to her. Yesterday, she thought, was a fluke. The sex was fast and good. Not to take anything away from his performance but when she thought it over this morning in bed, she was so turned on and it had been so long, she assumed it wouldn't have taken much to get her there. Today was

135

similar, but with one major difference. He was ferocious. Whatever his body demanded, hers instantly complied. If he had told her to bark like a dog, she wouldn't have thought twice about it. There was no way she was going to be able to look at him now, without seeing his lust coated expression as he growled her name. That was a complication, but one the more she thought about it, could be worked out. As long as they were on the same page.

Liv walked up to the table, set her purse down and took a seat.

Pulling a small notebook out of her purse, she avoided eye contact with Braden as she made his daily list, "You still wanna grocery shop?"

"Sure but a... We need to talk about something first."

The seriousness of his tone caused her to state, "No," as she started to make his list.

"Liv, twice now we've had unprotected sex..."

Jerking her head up, she glared at him, asking, "You got somethin'?"

"Like a condom?"

Narrowing her eyes, she snapped, "No dumbass, like an STD."

"Whoa! No! Not what I was tryin' to say."

"You sure? 'Cause I have just enough time to kick your ass and call the doctor's office before I go to work."

Holding his hands up, Braden replied, "I swear."

Nodding, Liv looked back down at the list, informing, "I get a birth control shot every three months."

She could hear the relief in his voice as he replied, "Cool."

"We done?"

Braden hesitated before saying, "Yeah. I'm good."

~

Staring at seven different types of lettuce, Braden had been in the grocery store for a good hour and still hadn't made it out of the produce section.

"Romaine," Charlotte stated as she stepped next to him.

Smiling wide at her, he questioned, "What?"

Rolling her eyes at him she laughed, "Liv likes Romaine. Lettuce."

"Thank you! I didn't think I was going to make it past the vegetables on her list."

Shaking her head at him, Charlotte held out her hand, saying, "Let me see."

Handing her his list, he asked, "What are you doing here?"

"I'm picking up your brother's roast for tomorrow night."

Pulling a pen out of her purse, she started writing on his list.

"Did you ask her out?"

"I did."

Smiling at him, she coaxed, "And?"

"She said no."

Appearing genuinely disappointed, Charlotte replied, "Awe, I'm sorry."

Shrugging off her sympathy, he assured, "Nah, it's all good."

"Really?"

"For sure. Its better this way."

With an understanding nod, she agreed, "Yeah, you're probably right."

"Thanks," he laughed as she handed him back the grocery list.

Charlotte walked away, looking back at him as she invited, "Dinner tomorrow at five thirty, okay."

"I'll be there." Braden replied before looking down at the list.

Laughing and shaking his head, he thought she was helping him. Instead she wrote, *'Roses are red. Violets are blue. I stopped by the shop to say hello to Liv. Somebodies putting it to her, and I'm betting it's you. ;)'*

Pacing in front of her door, Liv waited for Braden to arrive. After spending the first forty five minutes she was awake, lying in bed, thinking about the last two days, and her conversation with Charlotte when she stopped by the shop, she came to a decision. If she wanted mad, passionate sex, and Braden wanted to give it to her, then why the hell not. Charlotte had suggested setting a few rules for having sex without relationship type attachments. She'd get around to that. In the meantime, there were things she had never experienced and wanted to try. Braden was still all the things she needed him to be to make it through day to day life. This was sex. Just sex. It didn't change anything between them. It only meant a little redefining to their friendship.

Liv glanced at the clock, then down at herself. Her white fitted night tank fell right above the center of her thighs. Reaching down, she made sure her white tube socks with red rings around the top were pulled all the way up to her knees. An eager smile formed when she recalled him saying her socks were sexy. It was good he thought so because it was rare she went without them. Over the years, Liv had acquired forty two pairs of the exact same socks, to insure she always had a clean pair available to wear. She knew it was a bit odd, but there was something about knowing they were there in her drawer, that gave her comfort.

For a moment, she wondered if she should do something with her hair. It was brushed but a little wild without being fixed. Dashing to her bathroom, she felt pressed for time. He would be here any minute now. Sweeping her hair up into a loose bun, she did one last quick check in her bedroom mirror as she walk past it before hurrying back to the living room.

Before she made it back to the door it opened. Wanting to lunge at Braden, she fought the invisible pull, forcing herself to stand still.

"'Morning," he greeted, closing and locking the door behind him.

His coppery red hair wasn't combed back like it normally was. It was short in the back but the top was wild, messy and almost stood straight up all by itself.

She wanted to run her fingers through the front of his hair, but remained in place, repeating, "'Morning."

Narrowing her eyes at him, she watched a smile start at the corner of his mouth before it spread across his face. He wasn't going to move.

Braden was just under five feet away from her, heightening the anticipation. It was an interesting little game he was trying to play. One that she was sure would spark excitement if things started to get a little boring. However, simply waiting for him to arrive was all the buildup she needed, and if he thought he was going to win he was wrong.

With a smirk on her face, she informed, "I'm not wearing underwear."

The smile fell from his face seconds before Braden was right in front of her, pulling at her hips and kissing her relentlessly.

~

In the shower, Liv mentally checked off living room floor from her sex list. She liked the variety of locations but even up against her door the first day could still be somewhat considered missionary. As much as she disliked the idea, she was going to have to have a sex conversation with Braden. There was no good reason not to, but since she had been avoiding the subject for years with him, it made her feel uncomfortable. Sure, there was a joke here and there, for the most part, that was how she kept things on a friendship level. Not necessarily so she didn't think about him in that way, more so he wouldn't think she thought about him like that.

Liv walked up to the table while Braden was sitting there eating French toast and looking over his list. She couldn't keep herself from relishing the fact that he was eating her food. It was silly in a way. One of her favorite things about him was that she could tell he enjoyed eating what she cooked. He always bit off too big of a bite then took his time chewing. Almost like he couldn't wait to get the food in his mouth but once it was there he wanted to savor it.

Pulling the chair next to his out, Liv sat down and placed her elbows on the table. Folding her hands together, she rested her cheek against them, waiting for him to look over at her.

"What's up?"

"How experienced are you?"

With a confused smile he replied, "In..."

"Sex."

Setting his fork down on his plate, Braden shifted to face her.

"Why?"

Blowing out a loud breath, Liv griped, "Just answer the question."

"I haven't slept with a lot of women," he answered with an uneasy tone.

With a slight laugh, she replied, "Good to know. Not what I was askin' though."

Seeming a bit more at ease now, he admitted, "I don't know what you mean then."

"Positions, scenarios, locations, you know, experience."

~

It took Braden a good minute of Liv sitting there with eyebrows raised, and dead silence for him to comprehend what came out of her mouth. Acknowledging the fact that he didn't know much about her in that area, he couldn't help wondering why she was asking.

"Are you?"

"You really need to work on your conversation skills."

As things he'd like to do to her flashed through his mind, he could feel himself starting to sweat.

"I can't answer unless you do."

Giving him a dirty look, she blurted, "Why not?"

"I don't have anything to compare it to."

Glancing around, Liv appeared to be thinking things over.

Leaning back in her chair she was matter of fact as she stated, "Mostly in bed. I've done it in a car twice. Except for that, only in bed up until Monday. Missionary. Nothin' fancy."

He could feel his throat constricting as he tried to swallow. The palms of his hands started to ache. Needing to be filled with some part, any part of her.

Clearing his throat, the only thing he could get to come out of his mouth was, "Damn shame."

A smile broke out across her face as she offered, "I'm down if you are."

Pushing his plate to the center of the table, he reached over and pulled her out of her chair and onto his lap.

~

Standing by the stove next to Auggie, Braden thought about how backwards it was that the girls were in the living room waiting on dinner and the guys were in the kitchen preparing it.

"You rode with Liv?"

"Nah, we just got here at the same time."

Seth gave a curious expression as Braden confirmed, "Really, I'm not being sarcastic."

"How's the library comin'?" Auggie asked, opening the stove to pull his roast out.

Backing out of his way, Braden replied, "Slow, I spent all damn day at the grocery store yesterday, then the paint I ordered didn't match the curtain and..."

Seth started laughing as he closed the oven door behind Auggie.

"What?"

"He's cooking, you're grocery shopping and decorating."

Auggie looked up from his roast with a hard scowl before teasing, "Guess that means your gonna have to take up sewing."

Braden laughed, adding, "You never heard the saying real men crochet?"

"I think sewing and crochet are two different things..."

Patting Seth on the back, Auggie laughed, "You would know."

Seth's face turned a little red as they laughed and called the girls into the kitchen for dinner.

~

Once Penny and Seth left, Liv said it was time for her to take off and Braden saw no reason to stay either. After thanking them for dinner, because Auggie made the best roast he'd tasted in a while, he caught up with Liv at the end of the driveway.

"See you tomorrow," he assured, walking past her on the way to his car.

Lowering her voice, she shared, "We can pick back up Friday."

Swiftly turning, Braden felt panicked as he reminded, "It's Thursday."

"We're still on for beer and pizza."

Giving her a confused look, he shook his head at her.

"I'm pretty sore."

Braden's chest swelled at her words, "Oh yeah?"

Rolling her eyes with a smirk on her face, she replied, "Later," sliding into her car.

Turning back to his car, he opened the door and slid in.

There was no way he'd be able to hold out until Friday. Really, it was in her best interest, not to skip a day. Everyone knows sore muscles need to be worked out. Besides, she wouldn't be able to hold out either. He was going to make sure of that.

The farmhouse had been in Braden's family for generations. Passed down to Kieran, from his father. The Caffrey's were tradesman. Each sect had its own skill and for the most part they stuck with it. Kieran's bunch happened to be markers. The only people who ever saw the inside of the marking room were the markers, or a man set on permanently declaring their heart with a Celtic one on the left side of his chest. It was a Caffery tradition, one that had never left the farmhouse. That was until Penny took over the title, moved the marking room to her house and now here Braden was about to paint the ceiling purple.

As Braden leaned against the wall, staring at the old marking chair in the corner of the room, the one Penny wouldn't take because she said it reminded her of a dentist chair. He rubbed the left side of his chest. Liv called it his badge of honor in order to poke fun at him. Looking back, he had no idea why he wanted it so bad. He recalled falling in love with it the moment his mom showed him the lily drawn on a square scrap of paper. Even after Lily married Kevin, he kept it folded in his wallet. Carrying it with him for years until he had, what he thought at the time, was a reason to have Kieran place it on the left side of his chest. When he thought about it now, it was less of a reason and more of an opportunity that presented itself. Braden hated Lily and everything that came from his relationship with her. Except for his tattoo. There was a part of him that knew he was meant to have that mark. Brooks asked him once why he didn't get it covered up. That was honestly never a thought for him. Lily may have been the reason behind it but the crazy part was, she never even saw it. It was over between them, for the last time, before he'd had the chance to show her.

Closing his eyes, Braden shook his head at himself.

"You takin' a break?"

Surprised to see Liv standing in the doorway, he pushed off from the wall, questioning, "What are you doing home?"

"Penny has a doctor's appointment so we closed the shop for the rest of the day."

Smiling wide, he nodded, walking towards her.

"No."

Stopping in order to pout, he repeated, "No?"

He could tell she was having a hard time being firm with him as she held out her hand saying, "Get to work. I'll make lunch in about an hour."

~

Walking out of the doorway and down the hall into her room, she closed the door behind herself.

She kicked her shoes off and then stretched out on the bed. Liv wasn't a cold person, although she knew that's how everyone saw her. She just couldn't afford to be warm on the outside. People see too much of you when you're soft. You forget. You make mistakes. But if you let them know up front that you're hard, it isn't as easy for them to get to you. And when it turns out they didn't really want you after all, there's a comfort in that loss. They only had what was on the outside, anyway.

Smiling to herself, she closed her eyes, thinking of the way Braden made her feel. Deciding to skip today was the right call. Thursday's needed to be preserved. Besides, it wasn't like she lied. She was sore, but it was a good sore. Her muscles ached in the best way possible. Every time she moved, it reminded her of why. She could feel herself growing warm at the thought. The warmth she felt was simply a reaction to what he did to her body. He warmed her. Taking a deep breath, she recited in her mind, 'sex is not the same as making love'. She thought she was in love with him once. Now she knew better. This was sex. Back then she was young and naïve. She knew better this time.

~

The first coat of paint rolled onto the ceiling smoother than he thought it would. The guy at the hardware store had sworn it was all in the prep-work, he was right. Braden set his paint roller down onto the tray and walked to the kitchen.

After washing his hands, he walked back down the hall to Liv's door so he could ask her where to rinse out the roller. When he called her name and there was no response, Braden opened her bedroom door thinking she may have fallen asleep. Confused for a moment as he stared at her empty bed, his body caught notice before his mind did. His muscles stiffened and his palms ached. Her bathroom door was pulled to, not closed, and he could hear the sound of sloshing water. Liv was taking a bath.

For a moment he hesitated. In the scheme of right verses wrong, it was a clear invasion of her privacy. Then again, it wouldn't be the first time. Taking a step towards the bathroom door, Braden worked at containing his enthusiasm. The last thing he wanted was to run in there like he'd never seen a woman naked before. Even though, in all honesty, that was how he felt.

Slowly pushing the bathroom door open, the first thing he spotted were Liv's feet. Crossed at the ankle resting against the corner of the shower wall, her toe nails were painted almost the same color purple as he was painting the ceiling of her library. Braden's eyes followed her legs all the way to the tub. Making his way closer he saw her. All of her. With her colorfully tattooed arms crossed behind her head, only her face was above water. Her eyes were closed and her black hair seemed to be floating all around her. She was beautiful. So damn beautiful. His first impulse was to curse because her kind of beauty cut right through his chest.

Liv's poem entered his mind. As sexy as he found it the first time he read it, looking at her now, gave the words all new meaning. She reminded him of his first acoustic.

Braden's heart jolted in his chest as she opened her eyes. Startled in expression, she didn't move. She just laid there staring at him. His eyes wandered across her body once more, lingering on her luscious hips, tracing the curve of her waist to the soft round of her breasts. Almost back to her eyes, he noticed on the inside of her right arm was a simple black outline of a guitar, his initials making up the body.

As soon as his eyes met hers again, she sat up. Steam rose from her body as she stood. Dripping wet, naked and silent. She didn't say 'no,' fuss at him for being in there or make any snarky comments. This moment was a gift. He could have lunged at her, pushed her up against the shower walls and taken her. Instead he stood there silent with her, appreciating the moment.

Until he saw her shiver as goosebumps formed across her arms.

Grabbing both towels from the rack, he laid the first one down for her to step out on and held the second open for her to step into. Carefully drying her off, Braden walked her back. He folded the towel right at the small of her back, until she was up against the ledge of the sink. Smiling down at her, she looked worried. The look in Liv's eyes showed him more of who she was, than she had ever revealed. She never said it and he never noticed, but she was always worried, about everything and everyone. Leaning down he softly kissed her lips. This wasn't about him. It was about her and he wanted to show her that she didn't need to worry about this moment or any other one they shared.

It was insane the way he felt. All he wanted was to please her. Brushing Liv's damp hair away from her ears, he picked up her blue tooth ear buds off of the counter next to the sink. It was the first time in his life he wanted to give without anything in return. Braden slid the earbuds into her ears one at a time, placing a light kiss against her ear after each one. When her eyes started to question him, he pressed his lips against hers, and pulled away. Grabbing her phone from next to were her earbuds where, he opened her playlist.

Braden scrolled through her playlist and selected 'The Judge' by Twenty One Pilots. Liv's eyes lit up as he set her cell down and smiled. Gliding his hand down the curves of her body, he went down on one knee in front of her. As he glanced up at her, she bit her bottom lip, silently accepting his proposal. It had nothing to do with commitment to anything other than this moment. Rubbing his palms around her hips, if she was sore, he was going to make it better. Adjusting himself slightly, he lifted her leg over his shoulder. Leaning in, he passionately kissed her until she was gripping the sides of the counter, arching her back, shouting his name.

Desperately trying to focus, Liv stared at the checker board in front of her. She should have beat Braden by now. He was distracting her. How was she supposed to concentrate on beating him when all she could think about was running her fingers across his mouth, laying her hand against his forearm or tracing the lines on the palm of his hand. Earlier, when he touched her, it was more than a physical act. She was genuinely touched by him.

Blowing out a loud breath, Liv made her move and sat back. She watched Braden as he looked over the board with a smile. He moved his king one, two, three, four jumps in a row.

"I win," he shared before the realization of winning hit him and he jumped out of his seat, cheering, "I won! In your face! You lost and I won!"

Narrowing her eyes at him, Liv slowly stood up and walked to the kitchen sink.

Quickly behind her, he reminded, "That was only one game."

"I don't want to play anymore."

Laughing at her, he informed, "You are a terrible loser."

Whipping around, she assured, "No, I'm not 'cause I don't lose."

"Well ya did today!" Braden blurted with a huge grin, pointing his finger at her.

Far from amused, she gave him a dirty look and started placing dishes in the sink.

Grumbling to herself, she knew it was silly to get agitated over a stupid game of checkers. It was his fault that she lost. Him and his ridiculously sexy...everything.

Leaning against the counter next to her, Braden asked, "Whatcha doin'?"

"Loser washes the dishes. So, I'm washing the dishes."

Scooting closer, he corrected, "That was the rule when you were the winner."

"Alright, what do you want?"

Flashing a smile, he pulled her to him.

"I want to kiss you."

She couldn't stop herself from smiling as she rolled her eyes.

"That's what you want?"

Nodding, he replied, "Under a blanket, on the couch."

"Really..."

"Yes, ma'am."

Thinking it was an odd request, Liv agreed.

Settled on the couch with Braden under her purple blanket with black stars, she felt a delightful rush of serenity. His kisses were long and slow as his fingers slid in between hers. Holding both of her hands he pulled them to the center of his chest.

"Keep your hands here," he stated, in a low tone, releasing her hands.

Reaching around her waist, he urged her onto his lap. Kneading his hands into her hips he kissed her as she faced him. When Liv started to slide her hands down to his stomach, Braden grasped her elbows, pushing her hands back to his chest.

"Here," he reminded before wrapping her tight in his arms as he kissed her.

Unable to keep her hands still, she opted to go the other direction. Running her palms up the sides of his neck her fingers traced his jaw before resting on his cheeks.

"Let me take you in bed," he breathed against her mouth.

Liv froze in place.

Brushing his lips against hers, he added, "Slow."

A sharp pang of uncertainty caused her to drop her hands from his face as she shared, "That's not what this is."

"It could be."

"No."

~

Braden wanted to argue, but as he looked into her eyes he knew it was pointless.

She wasn't the same woman he was with earlier. The one that allowed him a glimpse of her vulnerable side, and softened under his touch. She was guarded.

Slowly letting go of her, he faked a smile, saying, "You should get to bed."
With a questioning expression, she shook her head.

"Your ass is mine, first thing in the morning."
Excitement flashed in Liv's eyes as she tossed the blanket off of herself, hopped up, and took off down the hallway to her room.

The second he heard her door shut, Braden leaned his head back. Staring at the ceiling, he thought about how lame she said her sex life had been. If she considered making love in a bed boring, then it was obvious she needed to be showed what it could be like. He wasn't entirely sure if he should be pissed at his cousin for sexually depriving her or thankful that he never put it to her like he should.

Deciding he had better get some sleep, he was serious about taking advantage of staying the night by having some first thing in the morning sex with Liv. When he lifted his head, she was standing in front of him. He started to ask if everything was alright. She seemed troubled, but as soon as he opened his mouth she leaned down and kissed him.

Liv's fingers tugged at the top of his hair as she practically violated his mouth with hers.

Before he knew it, the kiss was over and he was watching her walk away again as she said, "'Night."

"'Night," he repeated although he was almost certain she didn't hear him.

He took a slow deep breath. Stretching out on the couch, he was thankful. Definitely thankful.

The Dog House was packed as Liv and Braden squeezed in together at the bar. Wedged in between two couples; it was hard for him to keep his hands to himself. Every time she adjusted to keep from rubbing against him, he would shift and a try to do something with his hands. He tried placing them on the bar, in his pockets, behind his back. He did everything he could think of, short of just holding them over his head. As 'Hollow Moon' by Awolnation played overhead, Liv placed her hand on his shoulder. Her mouth was at his ear and he knew she had said something but it was lost the moment he felt her breath on his ear.

Tension filled his body as he turned to her, suggesting, "Wanna get out of here?"
Realizing that must have been what she said, she nodded with a laugh in response.

They told Auggie, they were going to take off before heading out of the bar and back into Braden's El Camino.

"Damn, I could hardly breathe in there." Liv shared as he pulled onto the road.

Unable to help himself, Braden teased, "'Cause it was packed or because of those tight ass pants you have on?"

Wide eyed, she turned to face him questioning, "You gotta problem with the jeans I have on?"

"I like it better when they're off."
Braden swerved as he glanced in her direction.

Lifting up off of the seat, she slid her jeans past her hips, asking, "You alright?"
His voice caught in his throat as he made a u-turn, heading in the opposite direction.

Liv tossed her jeans in the back seat before propping her feet up on the dash.

"Where are we going?"

Focusing on the road to keep from swerving again, he replied, "My place is closer."

"What do you think of this sweater?"
He could hear the smirk in her voice, prompting him to take a quick look.

"It's not my favorite," she shared, pulling it off over her head and tossing it into the back seat with her jeans.
Braden leaned forward slightly, grasping the steering wheel, hoping to make it home before her bra or underwear came into question.

Parked right in front of his apartment, Braden took his seatbelt off and turned to her with a wide smile.

"You comin' in?" he challenged, opening the driver's side door.

Liv appeared offended as she replied, "You think I won't?"

"This isn't the country," he warned, reminding her there would be spectators.

She seemed to be considering what he had said.

"You know what I discovered this week?"

Shaking his head, he thought about everything they had done.

"It's good to try new things," she informed with a smile.

Braden smiled back, then his jaw dropped as she swung the door upon and hopped out.

Leaping out of the driver's seat, he slammed his door shut, tripping over the curb as he pulled his hoodie off. She was halfway to his door before he caught her. Frantically covering her with his jacket, he pulled her the rest of the way to his door by it.

"Are you crazy?" he barked trying to get his key into the door.

Laughing at him, she assured, "I checked first. No one was looking."

Finally getting the door open, he shoved her inside scolding, "You're insane."

"Why? Because I walked to your door in my bathing suit?"

Turning to get a good look at her even though his hoodie was still draped over her shoulders, it was obvious now, she was wearing a bikini.

Somewhat relieved, Braden fussed, "You're an asshole, Liv."

"Ha!" she blurted before taunting, "Don't be mad 'cause I got you."

A slow smile spread across his face as he reached over and locked his front door.

"Now I've got you."

Biting her bottom lip, her expression quickly changed.

~

The look in his eyes was almost sinister. Reaching into his jacket around her, he took her arms and folded them across her chest. Lifting the sleeves of his hoodie, he tied them together across her chest, preventing her from moving her arms without a struggle.

Excitement exploded in her chest as he questioned, "You like to try new things?"

Nodding she let him lead her to the kitchen.

Kneeling on two kitchen chairs, with the seats facing each other, Liv was bent over the table. Her arms, imprisoned by his hoodie. She found herself clenching her fists, hugging them tight to her chest. Braden's arms encircled her shoulders and his face was buried in the back of her hair. Every push from behind pulled them both closer to the edge until neither one could hold back any longer.

Braden didn't give her any time to recover as he lifted her off of the chairs, pulling his jacket off of her while setting her on her feet. Passionately kissing her, it was a good thing he was holding onto her so tight. Her knees were weak and her legs felt wobbly. She felt disoriented. Off balance. Dragging her to the couch, Braden continued to kiss her as he flung them both onto it. Her back was pressed into the pillows as she lay on her side against him. Wrapping his leg around hers, he held her to him. Without letting up, he slid an arm around her waist, pressing her into him, while his other was at her jaw, holding her face to his.

Everything started to slow down. Her heart beat along with his kiss as she felt herself drift off.

~

Her lips were still moving, but just barely. The feel of them lightly brushing against his was almost too good to stop.

Afraid moving would wake her, Braden carefully scooted his head back. Wrinkling his brow, he looked at her. She was at peace. Her chest rose and fell against his as her hands remained tucked between them. This was what he was missing. It wasn't their position, he's been here before. It was a feeling. One that he couldn't describe, still he knew exactly what it was. She was feeling it too, he saw it in the little glimpses she gave him when her guard was down.

Braden leaned his forehead to Liv's and closed his eyes. Thinking about the night he found her drunk, passed out in the bathtub, he wished he would have told her about Kieran. She couldn't have been more broken than she was that night. Maybe if he had told her, she was mourning a man that wasn't worth a second thought, she might not be so guarded with him. Or it was possible between what he did to her in high school and her husband cheating on her, this moment wouldn't be happening at all. None of that mattered now. What mattered was, he was starting to realize, the things he thought he lost, were not half as good as the feeling of lying there with Liv.

'Come And Get Your Love' by Redbone made Liv's morning drive to work just a little bit sweeter as she tapped her fingers against the steering wheel and sang along with the words. The weekend had proved to be an amazing addition to a weeks-worth of Braden. Why Lily cheated on him, when they were dating, she would never understand. Aside from the fact that it was wrong and hurtful, that man knew his way around a woman's body. She had no idea sex could feel this way. It was as if he was able to draw every ounce of pleasure out of her body, at will. Liv was pretty well acquainted with the facts of life, but this week had taught her a new one. Not all orgasms are created equal.

The little bell above the door at Legacy Ink rang as she stepped into the shop. Noticing Penny and Jimmy at the counter, Liv greeted them both on her way to the back.

"What's up Jimmy?" Earned her a smile, while her, "Good morning, beautiful," brought an unexpectedly cautious expression to Penny's face. Liv figured she must have had an early call from Sarah or something. Penny was normally cheerful but lately the whole trying to make a baby situation had considerably taken its toll on her mood.

Liv tossed her purse on the chair in the back office, still humming the tune from the song in her car. There was an added feeling of warmth in her chest as her phone vibrated in her hand.

B: Ever had phone sex?

Pausing in the doorway, she replied to his text.

L: No.

B: No?

Holding back her smile, she texted.

L: No, I have not.

B: Oran has the hook up on that floor you wanted.

L: Cool.

B: I'm gonna ride with him to pick it up but it's gonna take all day.

L: Sounds good.

B: He'll deliver it tomorrow.

Excited about the wood floors for her library, she was curious what one had to do with the other.

L: Phone sex?

B: Yeah. I thought tonight. You down?

Biting her bottom lip, she texted back.

L: If you'll be UP.

B: Dirty girl.

Liv let out a laugh.

L: Later.

Sticking her phone in her back pocket, she gave up trying to wipe the smile off of her face and walked to the front of the shop.

Resting her elbows on top of the counter, she leaned against it.

"What's on the agenda for today?"

Penny appeared nervous as Jimmy replied, "Nothing."

"Then why are we here?" She laughed, thinking of heading back to her house and catching Braden before he left.

Cautiously Penny replied, "We weren't really sure what to do."

Shaking her head at Penny, Liv noticed Jimmy had a solemn expression on his face also.

"Am I missing something?"

Penny's eyes were sympathetic as she started to say, "Well... Last year..."

Liv's heart pounded in her chest. She glanced at the calendar and realized. She forgot.

A cold sickening feeling washed over her. Both Penny and Jimmy's eyes were sorrowful, but she couldn't help feeling as though they were judging her. She forgot.

"I'm out," she blurted, turning and walking back to the office.

Guilt tore through her soul as remorse over what she had done overwhelmed her. Grabbing her purse, she walked out of the back door. She swore she would never forget. She forgot.

~

Sitting on the center of his bed, Braden thought of different ways to get started. Should he call Liv? Or should it be over a text message. After deciding it should definitely be a phone call, he wondered if he should text her first. He had never done this before. It always seemed hot and since Liv wanted to try new things, he thought it would be something they could try out for the first time together.

With an eager smile he sent her a text.

B: Are you naked?

Staring at his phone, he waited for her to text back, when it rang. Instant disappointment washed over him when he saw the call was from Penny.

"Hello," he snapped hoping to quickly get her off the phone.

Penny didn't waste any time, questioning, "Have you heard from Liv?"

"I talked to her this morning. Why?"

"I've been trying to call her. She won't pick up."

A nervous feeling crept through his bones as he asked, "What happened?"

Sounding like she was about to cry, she replied, "This morning at the shop. She was in a really good mood but then she looked at the calendar. I figured she went home."

"I was with Oran all day," he griped, hopping off of his bed.

He could hear her sniffle as she offered, "I talked to Uncle Brennen, the cabin's ready if we..."

"Damn it, Penny. No. Just... Damn it."

Penny started to cry harder into the phone.

"I didn't mean to remind her. I didn't realize she forgot."

Tossing his cell down on his bed, he barked, "Hang on."

While pulling a t-shirt on over his head, he worked at not being angry with Penny. It didn't matter that he was pissed and he had told her to let it go. She was his sister and he hated to hear her cry.

Braden grabbed a pair of jeans from his basket of clothes and yanked them on.

He picked his phone up off of his bed and assured, "I'm going to go check on her. You don't need to cry. She probably just needed the day off."

"You didn't see her, Braden. She..."

Anger and fear twisted in the pit of his stomach as he cut her off, saying, "Alright, Pen, I get that she was upset."

"I'm sorry."

Balancing his phone between his shoulder and his ear, Braden sat on his couch putting his socks and shoes on as he repeated, "I'm going to go check on her."

"Okay." Penny replied in a soft voice, still sounding sad but thankfully no longer crying.

He stood up and grabbed his keys saying, "I'll call you back."

Without waiting for her to end the call, he hung up and headed out of his apartment door, hoping to find her in a better state than he did the last time.

The farmhouse was silent when Braden walked in. He wasn't sure if that was a good thing or not because Liv's car was parked outside. It was eerily quiet as he walked through. Deciding to start where he ended up finding her last time, he headed down the hall.

Walking past Liv's library room, he stopped. The light was on. Turning back, he remembered shutting the light off.

"Liv..."

She was sitting in the old marking chair in the corner. A bottle of liquor was in between her legs. There was a glass in her hand, as she rested both on the arm of the chair.

"I forgot," she shared before drinking what was in her glass.

The pain in the pit of his stomach twisted. It was painful to watch her as she held the glass next to her thigh and tipped the liquor from the bottle into it.

"That's when we met ya know... On his birthday."

Braden stepped closer to her as she emptied another glass in one swallow like it was nothing before repeating her refill routine.

"And I forgot."

Making the final step to be next to her, Braden wanted to knock the glass out of her hand and jerk her out of that damn chair. Maybe shake her a little.

So she forgot his birthday. Kieran forgot to be faithful. It was about even as far as Braden was concerned, and the fact that she was sitting there reminiscing or remorseful made him sick. It was different before; before she was grieving. She didn't need to grieve anymore. The man had been dead for a while now and she had him. They had each other. The agony of seeing her falling apart over someone who never deserved anything from her to begin with was too much for Braden.

He was going to tell her that Kieran was a cheating bastard. That he was an unfaithful piece of shit and that she needed to get over it because what they had was better. Her marriage to his cousin meant nothing compared to what was between them.

When he opened his mouth to speak, he stopped, hearing her admit, "I always hated this room."

Instead of talking, he decided to listen, watching her eyelids close then flutter open again.

"This chair... I was jealous... of a chair."

Liv lifted the glass and started to take another drink before he took it away from her. Even then, she wouldn't look at him.

"There was never anything for me...here."
She flinched as he touched her arm.

"Don't say that."

Her eyes remained closed this time as she reached for the bottle between her legs assuring, "It hurts to be wrong."
Braden pulled the bottle away from her. Liv was fixing to be out, there was maybe enough left for a half of a glass in her liquor bottle.

"Please... go."
Shaking his head, he touched the side of her face.

Liv's eyes opened as she looked into his, mumbling, "Away from here."
He watched her eyes close, thinking about what she said.

She would most likely be out for a while. Staring at her, Braden thought she might be right. He needed to get out of there, but so did she. If it was just the two of them, away from everything, she would see all they needed was each other. He couldn't very well take her without her permission, she'd be pissed, but he knew if he waited until she sobered up, there was no way she would agree to going.

Taking a long shot, he nudged her, asking, "You want me to take you away from here for a couple of days?"

When there was no response, he nudged her again. Liv's head fell forward, sort of like a nod. Close enough.

Braden walked out of the room and into Liv's. Opening her closet he dug around until he found a bag. She would need some clothes. Pulling her drawers open, it was a bit odd that the first three were filled with socks. Not a variety socks, identical pairs of the same socks. Moving on, he knew she needed underwear, clothes, and pajamas. Grabbing items and stuffing them into the bag he thought she would need deodorant. In the bathroom, he wasn't sure what else she needed. Toothbrush and toothpaste were a must, but there were twelve different types of lotion in there. Shaking his head he grabbed what he thought would be necessities and called Penny.

Penny picked up after only one ring.

"Braden, was she there?"

"Yeah," he replied before lying, "She's okay. She just wants to be alone right now ya know."

"I understand. She's okay though?"

Taking a moment to make sure his voice was convincing, he replied, "She needs some time to herself, that's all. She'll be back at the shop Thursday, but she doesn't want to talk to anyone until then. Okay."

"Okay, I'll tell Charlotte."

"Alright, Pen. Later."

Putting Penny's mind at ease also meant no one would expect to hear from her. Which was good. He left Liv's phone on her bed, intentionally, not packing it.

Now, there was the small problem of grabbing the things he needed from his apartment. And food, they would need food. If he put her in the car now, he could risk her waking up at one of the stops. What if someone saw her in his car at the grocery store? Braden needed to be smart about this in order to successfully get her out of town.

Opting to leave Liv at her house to run errands seemed like the best route to take.

~

When Braden arrived back at the farmhouse, and found her on the floor instead of in the chair where he left her, he felt a little bad for leaving her there. She didn't seem injured, although really how would he be able to tell until she sobered up.

He made a few trips back and forth out to his car before he decided on the best strategy of getting her in his car. The blanket they kissed under on the couch was on the passenger side and her pillow was in there too. That way, if she did start to come out of her stupor, maybe she would think she was at home. At least that's what he was hoping.

Braden lifted her off of the floor, flinging the top part of her body over his shoulder. He made it through the house and off of the porch before standing there staring at the open passenger door. It seemed fairly simple in his head. Sliding her off of his shoulder while holding onto her he was able to bend her over enough to get her in. Moving her into an up-right position he clicked her seatbelt on, and wrapped the blanket around her. He ended up rolling the window down so he could hold her head with one hand to keep from shutting her in the door. That actually worked out nice because he was able to wedge her pillow in between her and the door, so she could comfortably lean against it.

Sliding into the driver's side, he slowly rolled up the passenger window. Glancing over at her, he smiled. This was going to be good for her. For both of them.

Liv rubbed her eyes with her fingers tips, trying to alleviate the pain sunlight was inflicting on them. The stiff feeling in her body had nothing on the throbbing in her head. Confused, she couldn't figure out why it was so bright or where the musty mothball smell was coming from. Still half asleep and in a hangover daze, she slowly stood up.

Braden's voice came from somewhere, informing, "Bathroom's the door on your left." Stumbling into the kitchen, she could feel Braden's eyes on her as she squinted at her unfamiliar surroundings.

"Where the hell am I?"

His voice was calm as he replied, "Away."

For a second, she thought she might be dreaming.

"What?"

"Does it matter?" he answered, walking towards her.

Her squint turned into a glare. She needed to shower so she could wake up enough to be as angry with him as she needed to be.

The throbbing in her brain had turned into a dull ache after her shower. She refused to take aspirin simply because it was helping her keep an agitated state of mind. It didn't matter what he said, taking advantage of her drunken state by driving her out of town without her consent was for lack of a better word, a crime.

"When you take someone against their will, it's kidnapping."

Seemingly offended, Braden argued, "It wasn't against your will. You were unconscious."

"That's worse."

Shaking his head at her, he admitted, "You wouldn't have come any other way."

Wide eyed, Liv threw her hands out at her sides saying, "That's kidnapping."

"Look, we're here now, lets..."

Crossing her arms, she leaned against the wall stating, "No."

"We could..."

"No."

Stepping closer to her, he griped, "Would ya stop being pissed at me?"

Refusing to change her disposition, Liv asked, "Where's my phone?"

"I left it."

"Where's yours?"

With a heavy sigh, he replied, "Its put away."

"Then no."

Appearing frustrated, Braden fussed, "Fine. Be that way then. We're about fifty miles from nowhere, so funky ass attitude or not, you're stayin' here until I get ready to leave."

Pushing away from the wall, she stomped back to the couch and sat down.

Infuriated with him, Liv switched back and forth between refusing to look in his direction and giving him hateful glares. He must be losing his mind to think taking her to the middle of nowhere while she was passed out was a good idea. Maybe he had finally snapped. As long as she had known him he always seemed somewhat passive, even where Lily was concerned. Sure he would get upset but he was the king of sedentary response.

As she continued to sit there stewing, trying to figure out why Braden would do something this drastic, she glanced over at him. He was standing in front of two glass doors that opened from the center to the outside. The sun coming through them highlighted the copper color of his hair and the distressed expression on his face. She wanted to look away but she couldn't. She wanted to lock herself in the bathroom until he gave in and took her home but she didn't. Everything about this was wrong. Their pain, due to life's circumstances, was supposed to be shared. However, at the moment, she seemed to be the cause of his. That wasn't who she wanted to be. In her mind, she recognized the past week may have been an all good things come to an end farewell to their unusual friendship.

Yesterday she was sick with guilt but the longer she sat there drinking, the more it occurred to her, the things she was holding onto from Kieran were ridiculous. Liv had fallen fast and hard the moment she met him. When she looked back on her life with him though, it was somewhat mediocre. She loved him, and if he were alive today she would still be committed to him; holding out hope that things would change. It was all rather sordid and cliché when she thought about it.

Liv was smitten with a guitar player that was hung up on someone else. After their one night stand, she left town heartbroken, questioning her worth. When she came back overflowing with self-confidence, she thought he would take notice. She only came back to throw the woman she became in his face. And as it turned out, she found someone else and she didn't even care that he didn't remember her in the first place. It seemed now, everything had come full circle. Death had caused her another heartache leaving her questioning her worth. Liv was smitten with a man that used to play guitar that was hung up in life.

Getting up, she walked over to where Braden was standing. Liv stared through the glass doors at the trees and the leaves covering the ground.

"It's nice here."

"You still mad?"

Smiling to herself, Liv replied, "No, but I think you need therapy if you're into kidnaping people."

Braden cracked a smile before his expression grew serious again. "I hate that you miss him. Especially now."

Taking a deep breath, she knew he did.

"You of all people should understand."

"I don't miss Lily. I haven't in a long time."

Liv turned and looked at him, "It's not about the person, it's about the things you missed out on."

Nodding, Braden questioned, "This is it. Isn't it? I crossed a line."

Closing her eyes, she thought for a moment.

The same man who spent an entire week fulfilling every fantasy she had then kidnapped her was willing to let go just like that. It was the inevitable and she knew it too, but it saddened her that there wasn't the least little bit of fight in him. With all the things that Braden was, when it came down to it, he still wasn't man enough for her. Maybe there was no such thing.

The weight of the moment grew to be more than what Liv was prepared to handle.

Lightening the mood, she asked, "Do you starve your hostages? Or is there food here?"

"I got you covered," he assured as a smile spread across his face.

Walking to the kitchen, Braden opened the ice chest next to the pantry.

"We've got, frozen burritos, corndogs and toaster streusel."

Stepping into the kitchen, Liv replied, "Great. How are you going to cook 'em?"

Braden gave her a curious look before glancing around the kitchen. Liv couldn't help laughing as he kept turning in circles with a baffled expression on his face.

"There's no stove."

Letting out a loud laugh, she enlightened, "I hope you know how to make a fire."

"Guess that was poor planning on my part."

"I'm sure your next kidnapping will go much smoother."

Braden burnt one of his corn-dogs and lost another in the fire before Liv took control of heating them over the fire. It was only fair since he did build an excellent fire for them. This was his first time to have campfire corn-dogs, but he had to admit they weren't too bad.

There was a crisp chill in the air and although it was warmer next to the fire, it was colder than he expected. Alternating between holding his hands out towards the fire and rubbing them against his own arms as the sun started to set.

Grabbing his arm, Liv quietly warned, "Don't move."

Slightly panicked, he took a step back.

"Be still or you're going to scare it away," she fussed in a hushed tone while looking straight ahead.

Following the direction of her eyes, Braden saw a deer cautiously making its way through the clearing less than twelve feet away from them.

They watched the deer, as it stopped with a jerk and stared right at them. Liv's hands tightened around his arm as they stood there silent. Looking at her as she focused on the deer, Braden couldn't keep still. He wanted this to be the beginning of something, not the end. Reaching with his other arm, he placed his hand on the side of her face, gently turning her focus to him. When he leaned in to kiss her she let go of his arm and tilted her head away from his hand.

"We should put out the fire and go in," she stated, her voice causing the deer to dart off into the trees.

Braden knew she was right but that didn't lighten the sting.

"Just like that?"

Shaking her head at him, she questioned, "Just like what?"

"I gotta admit, Liv, I'm feeling a little used."

He wasn't. Not in the slightest but that was the second time she turned away from his touch and he wanted to piss her off. He wanted her angry, maybe even hate him a little. Because that was how he felt.

Liv appeared surprised at what he said before her expression settled into exactly what he was going for.

"How does it feel?" she asked with a hint of animosity in her eyes.

"I'm not gonna go off and dye my hair and get covered in tattoos."

Her hand quickly flew at his face catching him right on the outside of his eye.

His face burned but it felt better than the sting of her turning away so he egged her on, "Was it the longest revenge plot in history or you just wanted to make sure you were good enough to finally give it up to Pat?"

Another hard slap in the exact same spot brought Braden closer to reason.

"Hit me again," he growled at her, wanting the physical pain to out-weigh everything else.

Taking a step back, Liv held out her hands.

"You've got issues."

Braden could feel the emptiness returning as the cold air around them soothed the side of his face.

~

Standing there staring at the man in front of her, Braden seemed unfamiliar. He appeared sick with need. Liv could feel the anguish in his eyes creeping into her chest. It was painful and miserable. That was when she realized, it was how he must have felt when he found her drunk and in the bathtub that night. She was responsible for this. The hollowed despair had been temporarily filled by one another, only as long as they were together. They had used each other to stay broken and in pain. It was wrong.

There was nothing more to say as Liv walked to the glass doors. She hesitated but only for a second. Opening the doors, she went straight to the couch. Staring through the glass doors from the safety of the couch, she watched Braden put out the fire he built. He stood there staring at it until she could no longer see the flames. When there was only darkness on the other side of the doors, she heard them open and turned away.

Hearing Braden's footsteps, the familiar heal-toe swooshing sound stopped right in front of her.

"The only time I feel anything is when I'm with you."

Liv closed her eyes and shook her head. This was too much. The burden was too great. She looked up, but he was already gone.

~

Closing the door behind himself, Braden started to feel hot. His breathing picked up as he sat on the end of the bed. Pulling his shirt off he laid back against the bed until his head started to ache. It was time to surrender to defeat and lick his wounds. Sitting up, he grabbed his shirt and stood. She didn't want him.

The sting of reality weighed heavily on him as he turned to look in the mirror. Staring at his reflection, the area around his eye was pink and sore to the touch. An involuntary smile pulled at the corner of his mouth when he thought about her hitting him. He was being an asshole and he'd deserved it. His eyes wandered down to the mark on the left side of his chest. He deserved that too. A reminder of bad decisions, wasted time and opportunities.

He closed his eyes and took a deep breath. When he opened them, Liv was watching him through the mirror, cautiously walking up behind him. She reminded him of the deer they saw outside as he turned to face her. Stopping with a jerk, she froze in place, staring right at him, ready to bail at any second. Her focus wasn't on his face though. Liv's eyes were fixed on the lily that covered the left side of his chest.

Her eyes were open. Not because she was looking at him, because they seemed to be waiting for the answer to a question, that was yet to be asked.

"Don't." Liv breathed as Braden started to pull his shirt on.

Lowering his arms to his sides, he let go of his t-shirt.

Taking a step forward, she placed the palm of her hand against his mark, whispering, "Braden."

He had no idea what was happening. Liv seemed to covet the lily on his chest as she spread her fingers across it before resting her forehead against the center of his chest. Similar to when she slapped him, Braden's body burned at the feeling of her hand against him. Slowly, he reached his arms around her. Holding her to him, if she pulled away he felt as if she would pull his heart right out of his chest. She lifted her other hand up, resting it against the back of his neck in response. He wanted to say something but the silence between then was so beautiful, he couldn't bring himself to break it.

Tension swelled inside him as Braden leaned his head down and kissed the top of her head. As she slowly tilted her head back to look at him, he took advantage, placing a soft kiss on her forehead, her cheek and then against her lips.

"Take me in bed," she murmured against his mouth. "Slow."

Braden slid his hands to her sides and removed her shirt. The feel of her bare breasts brushing against his chest as he walked her back to the bed was almost too much for him. 'Slow' he reminded himself as he leaned her back onto the bed. Running his hands down her sides, his fingers glided against the curve of her waist until they stopped at her hips. He leaned down, following her waistband across her stomach with his lips. Unfastening her jeans, he slid them down her legs. He stared at her socks, almost leaving them behind, when the thought of her completely naked compelled him to push them down one at a time until her calves and feet were bare.

Standing up, he took a step back, removing his jeans and underwear as he gazed down at her. Completely naked with her eyes still open, she bit down on her bottom lip. The tension he felt was overwhelming as the word 'slow' echoed in his mind. Climbing on the bed, he hovered over her. She nodded as his eyes swore there was no going back from this moment. His lips met hers with passion and love as he sank down into her, relishing every sound and movement they created together.

She was the purpose in his meaningless life and although he still didn't quite understand, holding her against him as she slept after making love to her gave him reason.

The bitter sweet ecstasy of Braden moving against her in the morning light, pulled every one of Liv's emotions to the surface. He had woken her with soft kisses, caressed her body lovingly, until every part of her surrendered to him. They were tied to one another in so many ways, being bound to him like this only seemed natural. But they had already spent too much time relying on one another. Using the other to enable themselves, for it to last.

Another kiss proceeded by a smile followed by a touch that enticed a moan kept them in bed most of the afternoon. They were wasting time, killing time, savoring it and fighting it all at once. Inevitably time got the best of them and they packed up and headed home.

Braden carried her bag to the door once they reached the farmhouse. They hadn't said a word to each other the entire drive there. As Liv took her bag from him, she placed a hand on the side of his face and kissed him.

"Goodbye," she sighed, turning away from him.

There was no reply as she opened her door. Pausing for a moment, she pushed through her reservations, stepped into the house and closed the door behind herself.

Straight to her room, Liv dropped her bag on her bed and picked up her phone. Of course it was dead. Walking out of her room, she stepped into her half-finished library, sat down on the floor and cried.

~

Braden stood there staring at her door for a while before finally stepping off of the porch and getting in his car. She couldn't have really meant goodbye... But he knew she did. His chest hurt and he felt sick. He wanted Liv. The more he thought about her the more he knew, he'd felt this way about her longer than he'd realized. Without her everything that was holding him together was gone.

He'd spent his life being easy going, giving in and letting everyone else have their way. With no idea where to start, he had to find a way to keep her but he didn't know how. Charlotte instantly came to mind. She might be able to tell him what to do. Her and his brother's relationship was insane when it started, and somehow he managed to convince her to stay. She would know what it took to change a woman's mind. Plus, she was close with Liv. They were friends, and he was desperate.

Pulling up to The Dog House, it was Wednesday night and normally slow, he was glad to see not many people were there. Braden thought about going in through the back and going straight to Charlotte's office, but at the moment, having a beer first sounded better. When he reached the bar, Auggie had a pint of Guinness waiting for him.

"You alright?"

Shaking his head, Braden replied, "Nah, man. Pretty far from it."

"Need an ear? I've got two?" Auggie replied with a genuine look of concern.

"I was needin' to talk to Charlotte." Braden said just as she walked up.

With an interested smile, she questioned, "About what?"

Braden glanced at the scowl on his brother's face before deciding to just go ahead and confess to both of them.

"I've been messin' around with Liv."

Charlotte's eyes lit up as she turned to Auggie, gloating, "Told ya, now pay up."

Appearing disgruntled, he pulled out his wallet and handed her some money.

"Y'all were betting on my personal life?"

"Don't get all offended, it was just one little wager," she insisted before adding, "Oh, wait. Does she wear the socks when y'all... Ya know."

"Are you kidding me?" Braden griped in disbelief.

Frowning slightly, she sighed, "Sorry."

"So what's the problem?" Auggie asked.

"I took her to Uncle Brennen's cabin Monday night. We got back today."

They both stared at him, obviously waiting for the issue.

"She doesn't want to be with me."

Confused, Charlotte questioned, "Then why did she go away with you?"

"She didn't know we were going."

"How could she not know?"

"She was passed out when I took her."

Auggie instantly fussed, "You kidnapped her?"

Charlotte looked at Auggie teasing, "Does that sorta thing run in your family?"

"That was a pair of shoes. This is a person we're talkin' about here."

Sidetracked, Braden asked, "You kidnapped a pair of shoes?"

"And held them for ransom." Charlotte added.

Auggie turned to her and argued, "First off, you left them in my truck. Not kidnapping. Second Liv is a person. Which is an actual crime."

"You didn't drug her, did you?" Charlotte questioned in a concerned tone.

Growing agitated, Braden snapped, "No. She'd been drinking. Now can we move on?"

Taking a long sip from his beer, Braden questioned why he even tried talking to his family.

The look on Charlotte and Auggie's faces showed they were waiting for him to drop the bomb of 'I tied her up and left her in the closet for two days'.

"The problem is, I want her."

Charlotte gave him a sympathetic smile as she shared, "Sometimes people want different things."

Staring at her, that wasn't what he thought she would say. It was possible he wasn't explaining himself clearly.

"I want to be with her."

Sympathy turned to pity as she replied, "Braden, she may not want to be with you."

"Look, man, sometimes sex is just sex." Auggie said trying to emphasize his wife's statement.

"It's not that way with her," he insisted.

Braden knew Charlotte was just trying to make him feel better at this point by saying, "You're a relationship guy. Maybe she's not a relationship type girl."

"She was married for like ten years," he argued, not understanding why they were making this so difficult.

"Maybe that was enough for her."

Pushing away from the bar, he didn't want to hear anything else either of them had to say.

All he wanted was a little advice. Something to keep his spirits up. A word or two to urge him on. That all hope wasn't lost. Why did he expect good advice? They didn't understand. No one did. Except Liv.

Sitting in his car, Braden stared at his phone. He wanted to call her. No, he wanted to drive to her house and kick in her door and tell her it wasn't goodbye. With a heavy sigh, he decided to send her a text.

B: Am I fired?

He was surprised when she immediately responded.

L: I appreciate everything. I'll send your money with Penny.

B: I don't want your money.

It took a few minutes for her to respond.

L: I'm not giving it to you. You earned it.

Getting to the point, he didn't care about her library or her money, he wanted to see her.

B: Tomorrow is Thursday.

Braden sat in his car, staring at his cell, in disbelief.

L: It's just another day.

A slow day at the shop gave Liv time to reflect on what took place between her and Braden at the cabin. While Penny worked on her sketches, and Jimmy setup an online ad for help, Liv sat there visualizing the lily on Braden's chest. Yesterday she was sad, heartbroken even, but today she wanted to be mad. The problem was, she wasn't sure who she should be angry with. Kieran for giving the tattoo, Braden for receiving it, or herself for letting it get to her.

The bell at the top of the shop door rang, causing Liv to sit up and take notice of who walked in the door.

"How goes it Jimmy?"

"Pat."

Looking him over, Liv thought Pat looked good, but not as good as he did before last week.

Without greeting him, she ordered, "Jimmy, go get the checkbook out of my office."

Jimmy gave Pat an almost delightful smile before turning and walking to the back.

Making his way over to Liv, Pat looked down on her with a questioning expression.

"What's up?"

Pat appeared disappointed as he replied, "Guess nothin' today."

Nodding, she put on her best smirk saying, "It's just that way sometimes."

Penny's voice interrupted their conversation as she informed, "Braden said text him back or he's coming up here," from her corner across the shop. Liv started to smile at Braden's aggressiveness, then quickly caught herself as she glanced at Pat.

"Guess I can't beat those Caffrey's, huh," he remarked as he turned and walked out.
This was the second time since she'd known Pat, she blew him off for someone else.

Irritated because now she felt bad on top of the way she was already feeling, Liv stood up.

"Tell your brother, I'll have Jimmy kick his ass right back out if he comes in here."

"Are you serious?" Penny replied as if she wanted to laugh.

"Damn right I am!" Liv snapped, passing Jimmy on the way to the back.

Continuing to the office, she heard Jimmy say, "I couldn't find the checkbook."

"'Cause it's not in here," she said to herself as she stepped into the room and sat down.
Although it wasn't the worst day of her life, it was far from being a good day, and it sucked even more that there was nothing to look forward to."

~

There was no point in making pizza. It was just her. Sitting at her kitchen table, playing solitary, Liv sipped her drink. She tried listening to her music but every song only made her feel worse. Wondering if this was what her life was going to be like, solitary, her phone vibrated with a text.

B: Can I come in?

She tried to ignore his text like she had been all day, but this particular one gave her cause for concern.

L: No.

Waiting to see if he would text back, she wanted to check and see if he was outside. Did he really show up after she told him not to? If he was, something had changed. This was different.

B: Don't say no.

Liv felt a certain excitement in her curiosity as she hopped up and walked to the door.

L: Why?

B: I can feel you thinking about me.

That wasn't possible. Was it?

L: No.

B: Invite me in.

L: No.

Her breathing picked up along with her heart rate as she waited for his next text.

B: I have the key. I could come in anyway.

Refraining from making a joke about him kidnapping her, Liv held strong.

L: Go home.

B: No.

This was exciting her way more than it should have.

L: No?

B: I'm counting to 3.

L: So.

B: 1

L: GO HOME!

B: 2

Liv's stomach lurched in anticipation.

L: Braden.

B: Liv.

L: Stop.

B: I can't.

L: Please.

B: 1

Standing there staring at her door knob with her heart beating in her ears, she waited to see if he would really do it.

The door remained closed and locked. Disappointment set in. Liv started to open the door herself, then decided against it. She had called things off between them and it was the right thing to do. This was a test to see how strong her will was. They were bad for each other and if she opened the door, she would just continue to enable him.

Blowing out a loud breath, she turned around to get back to her game of solitary.

"I was at the back door."

Braden was there, in her house without permission. Liv had no idea what to say as he made his way towards her.

"You gonna get Jimmy to kick my ass outta here too?"

All she could do was lean her shoulders back against the door as her body called for him to come closer.

His hand molded to the shape of her hip as he rested his other on the side of her neck, whispering, "You don't have to pretend with me."

"We're not good for each other," she insisted, trying to let reason outweigh feeling.

Braden's lips drug across her jaw to her mouth as he suggested, "Let's be bad then."

Shaking her head, she replied, "That's not..."

"Don't argue Liv. This is what it is. It can be fast or slow but its real and I'm not letting go."

That was the last thing he said to her before she caved; before she broke down and gave herself away.

Yesterday, when Liv refused to answer his texts, Braden called Seth hoping he had better advice than Charlotte and Auggie. He advised him to do something unexpected. He did, and it worked. Braden woke up in Liv's bed feeling her lips against his skin. It wasn't a melancholy experience like at the cabin. She was smiling and it was genuine.

She was a morning adventurer, exploring and staking her claim on him in the sexiest ways possible. A deep throaty laugh would spill from her lips every so often, one he had never heard from her before. He gripped the sheets, held onto her hair and even cursed out loud once at what she was doing to him.

Sliding up, she kissed the center of his chest and then his lips.

"You've been holding out on me."

Rolling onto her back, she questioned, "You don't remember? Highlighted on my kindle?"

"You know when my fifth grade teacher told me, 'reading is fundamental,' I really thought she was full of shit."

With a satisfied expression, she laughed.

Taking advantage of her good mood, he placed his arm around her waist and suggested, "So... Fairmont's?"

"No," she replied, but with a smirk on her face.

Braden wanted to question her answer but pulled her to him for a kiss instead.

As he wrapped his leg around hers, holding her to him, she offered, "You can pick me up at eight for The Dog House."

"Did you just ask me out on a date?" he questioned with a wide smile.

"No."

"No?"

"We're just going together."

"Like steady?"

Liv let out a laugh before giving him a kiss.

~

Sipping a beer in Charlotte's office at The Dog House, Liv kicked her feet up on the chair next to her.

"Are y'all going to move in together?"

"I haven't thought about it." Liv replied, before sharing, "Kieran and I did."

"Did you tell him about his tattoo?"

"I haven't thought about that either."

"Really?" Charlotte questioned with surprise.

"Okay, I've thought about it. But not telling him."

"Why not?"

Shrugging she informed, "I don't want him thinking its fate or something like that."

With a light smile Charlotte asked, "Did you ever think maybe it is?"

"That would mean everything that's happened between us is based on a lie."

Nodding, Charlotte replied, "I get what you're saying. Isn't it going to be hard on you, though? Keeping something like that from him. Don't you think he has the right to know?"

Liv gave a heavy sigh, saying, "It's only ink."

"Seriously? You know that's not true." Charlotte snapped as her office door swung open.

~

Braden's stomach felt tight and his head was already starting to hurt as he looked at Liv sitting there in the chair. When Pat called him, he thought it was going to be to tell him to come back to work. It wasn't.

He stepped in leaving the door open.

"Charlotte, can you give us a minute?"
She didn't appear happy about it but she got up and walked out, closing the door behind herself.

Standing up Liv questioned, "You got a problem?"
Trying to figure out how to tell her, he had the awful feeling that it wasn't going to end well. What was he supposed to do though? Pat said he

was on his way to tell her. Not only that, he was going to tell her that Braden had known all along.

Swallowing hard, he started to confess, "The night Kieran died..."

Her face instantly fell into an unhappy expression.

"His phone was recovered."

Liv appeared confused as she shook her head. Obviously, not understanding why that was an issue.

"We went to the station and picked it up, so you wouldn't see it."

He could sense, she was starting to get the picture as she questioned, "Why is that?"

Shifting his eyes to the floor, Braden couldn't look at her.

Shoving him back against the door, she shouted, "Look at me! Look at me when you tell me!"

"He was seeing someone."

She stood there staring at him, her eyes lit up with anger.

"Who's we?"

"Liv, I..."

Her voice was slow and slightly frightening as she demanded, "Who is we?"

"Me, Auggie, Seth and Jacks."

With a short nod, she pushed him to the side, pulled the door open and stormed out.

~

Fury mixed with hurt in an almost blinding rage as Liv pushed through the swinging door into the main area of the bar.

Swiftly walking behind the bar, she gave Auggie a slight shove as she shouted, "Why?"

Charlotte turned looking past Liv at Braden as she questioned, "What's going on?"

"Yeah, what the hell?" Auggie questioned, looking down at Liv.

"I had to tell her."

Auggie's eyes narrowed as he scowled at his brother.

Before Charlotte could question what was going on again, Liv was in Auggie's face, "You knew Kieran was cheating on me!"

Liv heard Charlotte snap, "What?"

Focusing on Auggie's scowl, Liv shouted, "How long? Huh? Was there always someone else? How long did your lyin' ass cover for him?"

Running his hand down the front of his beard Auggie shook his head swearing, "I found out the night he died, like everyone else."

"Not everyone." Liv spit out at him before hearing Charlotte scold, "Augustus."

She had to get out of there and away from everyone.

Making her way out of the bar, she saw Penny and Seth walking in.

"Where are you going?" Penny asked with a curious expression.

Unable to look at Seth, Liv replied, "Sorry, beautiful, but your family has a real problem with the truth," as she continued out of the doors.

She was done and over this stupid town. She should have never come back.

"Liv, wait!" Braden called behind her.

Whipping around, his betrayal was the most hurtful.

"Why didn't you tell me?"

His voice was pleading as he replied, "I wanted to."

"But you didn't. You let me cry over him knowing. You knew."

He started to speak but she wouldn't allow it.

"I never should have come back here."

Reaching for her, he raised his voice fussing, "Don't say that."

She started to back away from him.

Grabbing hold of her, he swore, "I'm in love with you."

Shaking her head at him, that was what was hurting her the most.

Liv jerked out of his hold.

"Sorry about that, cause I'm not in love with you."

She was trying to hurt him. Hoping her words cut right through his heart.

"You're a liar."

Scoffing at him, she snapped, "I'm a liar because I won't tell you what you want to hear?"

"No, you're a liar because that's not the truth and we both know it."

"Wanting something to be true doesn't make it the truth."

"Denying the truth doesn't make it any less true, Liv."

"The only thing that's true about you and I is that the sex was hot."

"That's not all it was to you."

Braden was right. She was a liar. That didn't stop her though.

"The truth is, I wanted to get off and you were the only one here. You would have known that from the beginning had you asked why I wanted you."

She had to make him feel what she was feeling. Needing him to feel betrayed and hate the love he felt for her.

Without waiting for his response, she turned away from him. Pat happened to be walking towards her, giving Liv a sense of relief that she could get a ride home.

"Can you take me home?" she asked without stopping.

Instantly moving in the same direction as Liv, he assured, "I'll take you anywhere you want go," as he placed his arm around her shoulders.

Standing outside The Dog House, Braden's breaths grew heavy. He had to wonder if she was telling the truth. It wouldn't be the first time he misjudged a woman's feelings for him. He wanted it to be a lie. But if it was, she never would have walked off with Pat.

Braden walked back into the bar. There were too many people in there. Wading through the crowd was making him sick. He could feel himself starting to hyperventilate. He pushed through the swinging door into the back.

There was no levity in the back as he heard Auggie say, "We thought we were doing the right thing."

"Well you thought wrong didn't you." Charlotte confirmed as Penny spoke up, admonishing her own husband. "I expect this stupidity from my brother. You know better."
Braden hung his head. Everyone was feeling the fallout of what they had done.

He was about to walk out of the back door when he heard his brother say, "We were wrong." Angry with him, Braden stepped into the back office.

Heated, he shoved his brother as soon as he walked in.

"We were wrong? It was your idea."

Auggie shoved him back griping, "No one forced you."

"Like I had a choice." Braden spouted, turning to walk out.

Grabbing him by the front of his shirt before he could, Auggie barked, "You did, but you have to have a mind of your own to make one."

"Get off me!" Braden snapped, pushing his brother off of him.

"Why'd you tell her now? After all this time? She never would have found out."

Anger swelled in Braden's chest as he shouted, "Pat was gonna tell her!"
Before he could move, Auggie grabbed hold of him again.

He could hear everyone else in the room shifting around as his brother pushed him into the wall, holding him against it.

"That's why you told her?" Auggie growled. "You hurt her instead of standing up to Pat's stupid ass?"

"We hurt her." Braden defended, trying to push his brother off of him.

Pulling him off of the wall, just to shove him back into it, Auggie barked, "No! We screwed up trying not to hurt her. You hurt her tonight. This is on you."

His brother's words rang through his head causing wretched pain in the pit of his stomach.

"Hit me or get the hell off me!"
Auggie appeared tempted for a moment, then slowly let go.

With his family staring at him, blaming him for something that he wasn't the only one guilty of. He couldn't take it. Braden thought 'to hell with them' he needed to make things right with Liv.

~

The farmhouse was dark and silent when he arrived. Liv's car was there, but she wasn't. He tried her cell, but his calls when straight to voicemail. She left with Pat and it was clear, he was more than just a ride to her. Braden had lost.

Sitting on her couch, he thought about what she said outside the bar. Comparing it to what he woke up believing that morning, his cell phone rang. He didn't recognize the number as he let it ring. When it stopped then called again, he thought her phone may have died and she was trying to reach him.

He answered, "Hello?"

A woman's voice that sounded familiar, but he couldn't quite place, replied, "Braden? Can you hear me?"

"Yes?"

She sounded relieved saying, "Thank goodness. Braden this is Mrs. Strouse."

It was Brooks' mom.

"Ma'am."

"Mr. Strouse and I are in the middle of the Caribbean. The ship captain just notified us that Brooks was in a car accident. Can you please go check on him for us."

"Mrs. Strouse, I..." he started to politely decline before she pleaded, "I know you two had a falling out, but please. There is no one else for us to call."

"Yes ma'am," he agreed, unable to say no to the people he used to consider his second family. Braden and Brooks had been friends since the seventh grade, up until a few years ago. They were like brothers. That was before though, before Brooks cheated on Penny with Lily. Braden was actually a pretty forgiving guy but when it came to his sister being hurt, there was no such thing. And the fact that it was with Lily, just added insult to injury where both he and Penny were concerned.

All Braden intended to do was go in and make sure Brooks was still alive. When he saw him, lying in the hospital bed, cut up, bruised and with his shoulder in a sling, he was pissed. Not only because he had not seen him since the night their friendship ended, but because Brooks could have died and they weren't friends anymore.

Appearing surprised to see him, Brooks winced as he tried to sit up.

"How'd you know I was here?"

Keeping his tone short, Braden replied, "Your mom called."

"Guess she forgot we weren't friends." Brooks said with a hopeful smile.

"She didn't forget, she said there was no one else to call," he replied hoping it stung.

With slight frown Brooks nodded. "Lily does have that effect."

"Why the hell did you sleep with her?" Braden surprised his own self with his outburst.

"What can I say, she talks a good game." Shaking his head at his former friend in disgust, he turned to walk out.

"I really don't know what I was thinkin' getting with her. Penny was so awesome."

Making his way back to Brooks' bedside, Braden assured, "She still is."

"It didn't last long, ya know. Lily and me."

Full of contempt, Braden blurted, "Shocker." The room was silent for a moment.

"Thanks for comin'. I guess."

Braden started to walk out again then stopped, "Are they keeping you overnight or what?"

"Yeah, for observation."

Nodding, he replied, "I'll be sure to tell your mom."

Making sure he knew it wasn't because he cared, although a small part of him did.

In the hospital parking lot, Braden paused, when he saw the brunette that had caused most of the trouble in his life heading towards him. He clenched his fists at the sight of her, thinking, 'of course'.

Lily's expression was sweet as always, in a conniving way, as she greeted, "This is a surprise."

"An unpleasant one," he assured, letting her know there was nothing good about seeing her.

"Oh don't be mean, from what I hear, you're... fine."

He couldn't help wondering what could have been if it weren't for her.

"No thanks to you."

Flipping her hair off of her shoulder, she laughed.

"I'm glad you think destroying my life is funny."

There was absolutely nothing redeemable about her.

"I didn't destroy your life. Those were the choices you made."

"You lied to me," he stated, finding it hard to believe that she was being serious.

Shrugging a shoulder at him, she gave a light smile. "People sometimes lie."

"You swore you loved me."

The smile vanished from her face as she replied, "I did love you."

Braden couldn't help feeling a hint of joy at her irritated expression.

"You know you can buy into blaming me and all that your family spews about what a terrible person I am. All the horrible things I did to their precious little Braden, but you and I both know, I wasn't the only one at fault."

"You were screwing Keven," he reminded, almost finding it humorous that she had bought into her own lies.

"That's right and every night you were off making love to your music."

It was nice of her to bring that up. Another reminder of what she'd done to him.

"I missed out on a great opportunity because of you."

"You can tell that lie all day long, but if you had wanted it, you would have gone no matter what I said."

As always, she did talk a good game. He knew better than anyone, he had bought into it for years.

Braden stood there wondering why he was wasting his breath on her. He had already given her a large portion of his life.

"Anyways, I thought you should know. You can have your house back."

"How generous of you."

"It was generous. We were never late on the mortgage. Not even once."

Shaking his head at her, she really was something.

"Keven got moved up state. He's going to counseling. And so am I. We've both made a lot of mistakes but we're working it out."

"Fascinating."

Lily started to walk off then stopped.

"Would you like to know why I married Keven and not you?"

"Thrill me."

"He wanted me. That's all I ever wanted. I only wanted to be wanted. I wanted you. I loved you. I wanted to be the most important thing in your life, but I was always second."

He was so angry with her for trying to make what she'd done his fault, he could feel himself starting to sweat.

"Oh, and good luck with your new Lily, maybe things will work out for you better this time." Lily said as she continued on her way and into the hospital.

What the hell was she talking about?

Shaking his head as he walked to his car, he thought, Lily and Keven deserved each other.

Standing on the cobblestone walkway, Liv stared at the grey house with maroon shutters. She was exhausted but she knew the man inside would want answers. He always came across as accusatory. Not unkind just straightforward.

After her fight with Braden, Pat had taken her straight home, but the moment she stepped inside, she couldn't stand being there anymore. There was nothing left for her at the farmhouse or in that small southern town. In hindsight, she wished she had hopped in her car and drove, but her mind was so clouded. Flying seemed like a better idea at the time. The flight was actually a blur at this point. All she remembered was listening to 'Scars' by Papa Roach through her earbuds, and trying to get Braden off of her mind.

Liv knocked twice before a man with varying shades of silver in his hair and beard answered the door.

"If it isn't my wayward girl."

It felt better to see him then she thought as she smirked, saying, "I come by it honestly."

"That you do," he said in a gruff voice that was softened by a smile.

Stepping back, he opened the door wider to let her in. The house smelled familiar giving her a sense of home, even though she never lived there with him.

Romeo Vera looked exactly the same as he always had, with the exception of the over-abundance of gray he now had. It was slicked back, long on top, cut high and short on the rest of his head. His beard was long but always well maintained. Although he didn't sport full sleeves like his daughter, his forearms held their fair share of tattoos.

The smell of coffee wafted through the air as Liv made her way into the kitchen.

"It's got chickaree in it." Romeo cautioned as she pulled a cup out of the cabinet.

Pouring herself a cup, Liv asked, "You still retired?"

"I do the odd job here and there."

With a smirk Liv questioned, "Depending on what she looks like?" as she leaned against the counter and sipped her coffee.

Agreeing with a laugh, he asked, "You need money?"

"No."

"You in trouble?"

"No."

"Runnin' from the law?"

"No."

"Man troubles?"

Liv paused before laughing, "Man troubles?"

Romeo took notice, questioning, "What happened?"

"Nothing."

In a harsh parental tone, he stated, "Lillian." Cringing at the name, she automatically narrowed her eyes at him.

"Still going by Liv? Figured you'd of grown outta that."

"Nope," she replied with a serious expression. Taking a sip of his coffee, he nodded at her.

"How long you stayin'?"

"Until I find someplace else to go."

Romeo nodded again, saying, "Might be good to have you around for a while."
Thinking it might be, she smiled at him.

"I'll be in the shed out back if you need me. Get some rest, you look like shit."
Liv's smile grew wider as Romeo left the kitchen. It was good to be home.

Instead of going back to his apartment, Braden stayed the night at the farmhouse. It was wrong and he knew it but he wanted to be there the second Liv got back. That way he would know without a doubt, she was telling the truth.

It was around three in the afternoon, Liv still hadn't shown up, and Penny stopped by.

"What are you doing here?" she questioned as he let her in.

Braden repeated, "What are you doing here?"

Penny appeared hesitant to tell him as she replied, "Liv asked me to stop by."

The thought of her spending the weekend with Pat made his stomach turn.

"Why?"

Glancing away from him, she answered, "She just wanted me to check the house."

His anger flared as he questioned, "For what? For me? Does she wanna make sure I'm not here when she gets back?"

Penny frowned, saying, "She's not coming back."

Feeling as if his chest was tearing in two, he sat down on the couch.

Staring down the hall at her bedroom door, he couldn't seem to get past the pain he was in.

"She's moving in with him?"

"Who?"

Braden couldn't look at his sister as he replied, "Pat. She's moving in with Pat."

"I don't think so."

Braden could hear the confusion in her voice.

"Then where'd she go?"

There was a pause before Penny replied, "Up north."

Shifting his focus to his sister, he asked, "Where?"

"She doesn't want you to know," she answered before taking a seat next to him on the couch.

He couldn't believe she left town. She left him.

An over powering sense of dread filled him at the thought of never seeing her again.

"Braden." Penny said in a soft voice.

The pain was unbearable. Quickly standing up, he stormed out of the house.

~

Braden parked his car and got out. Swiftly walking up to the Shady Acres Golf Course, he passed the club house and walked straight onto the green. He could hear shouts and complaints from nearby golfers but he didn't care. He knew Pat would be there. The golf course was a Saturday ritual for Pat. He just had to find him.

Spotting Pat at the seventh hole, he kept a steady pace until he reached him. Pat took notice and stopped as Braden interrupted his putt. Before he could open his mouth Braden punched him in his right eye. More shouts and complaints echoed in the background. He still didn't care. At the moment, the only thing Braden cared about was kicking Pat's ass. Swinging again, and again, Braden continued punching him until he himself was face down on the green with his hands handcuffed behind his back.

~

After declining the option to make a phone call, Braden sat on a metal bench in a holding cell at the city jail. His knuckles were red and swollen and his hand ached from hitting Pat numerous times in the face. He wanted to feel better, feel like he'd at least accomplished something or achieved some sort of payback. Unfortunately, as good as it felt in the moment, beating Pat's ass wasn't going to bring Liv back.

Leaning his back against the wall, he hung his head and closed his eyes, when he heard the jailer holler to him.

"Caffrey, let's go."

Standing up, he shook his head.

"Come on, Judge Stevens came all the way up here on a Saturday evenin' to set your bail. Don't make him wait."

The jailer opened the holding sell and Braden followed him down the hall to a door on the left.

Instantly irritated, he saw Brooks sitting there talking to a man who he assumed was the judge.

"What are you doin' here?"

Brooks stood, saying, "Judge Stevens is a friend of my dad's."

His arm was no longer in a sling and he didn't look nearly as bad as he did in the hospital the night before.

"And?"

"Come on, man, I'm just tryin' to help."

Furious, Braden swore, "I don't want your help."

"To bad." Brooks insisted before sharing, "Just because you stopped being my friend, doesn't mean I stopped being yours."

"What kinda stupid ass..." Braden started before the jailer cut him off, reprimanding, "Want me to take you back to the holding cell?"

"Yeah." Braden snapped, not wanting to accept his ex-friend's help.

Judge Stevens spoke up scolding, "Son, you should be a grateful to have a friend like him."

Clearly the judge had no idea what he was talking about.

"He's not my friend."

Brooks stepped in front of Braden, griping, "I am your friend."

"Cheating on my sister with my ex? Yeah, you're a great friend." Braden mocked giving Brooks a little shove.

Brooks shoved back and before the judge or the jailer could stop them they were rolling around on the floor swinging on each other.

~

Sitting in the holding cell, Braden was now handcuffed to the metal bench. Brooks sat on the opposite side with his arms crossed tight against his chest.

"Penny forgave me, why can't you?"

Braden glared at him griping, "Like hell she did."

Turning towards Braden, Brooks swore, "Yes she did. A few months after she got married."

His glare turned into a curious stare as Brooks continued.

"I ran into her at The Store. She even hugged me."

Shaking his head at himself, Braden said, "How could you sleep with her?"

Shrugging, he replied, "Bad judgment."

Braden started to laugh, that about summed up his own relationship with Lily.

As a new jailer came on shift, Braden started to wonder if he'd blown his chances of getting out before Monday. He was about to ask for his phone call when the jailer walked up to the holding cell.

"Strouse."

Brooks looked at Braden before hesitantly standing up.

"You want out or what?"

"Is Judge Steven's still here? I came to bail him out." Brooks explained pointing at Braden.

Before the jailer could answer, Braden rolled his eyes hearing his brother's voice.

"What in the hell is wrong with you?" Auggie questioned with a scowl.

"Sir, you can't be back here," the jailer fussed before his radio went off with a voice assuring, "I cleared him to go back."

"Braden jerked against his handcuffs griping, "You bailed Brooks out and not me?"

"You and I are going to have us a talk," Auggie replied before telling the jailer, "Let me in there."

Appearing shocked that Auggie was giving him orders, he assured, "No one is allowed in the cell unless they're arrested and booked in first.

With an irritated scowl Auggie gave a loud sigh before offering, "Alright then. It's you or him."

The jailer stared at him in disbelief as Brooks, questioned, "What?"

When the jailer took a step back, Auggie turned and punched Brooks in the face.

Brooks fell backwards into the wall holding the side of his face.

"What the hell, man!" he shouted at Auggie.

"Like you didn't have that comin'." Auggie fussed before walking down the hallway with the jailer close behind him.

~

Braden was still handcuffed to the metal bench in the holding cell. Now, he was stuck in the cell with his brother sitting next to him.

"Got anything to say for yourself?"

Giving Auggie a stupid look, he replied, "Yeah, but I'm handcuffed and you're not. It would hardly be a fair fight."

With a hard scowl, Auggie griped, "Fine, I'll go first."

With a disgruntled expression, Braden waited to hear what his brother had to say.

"Do you know what I did when I thought I'd lost Charlotte?"

"Got good and drunk?"

Shaking his head, Auggie shared, "No, smartass. I cried."

Rolling his eyes, Braden replied, "Oh bullshit."

His face was sincere as he swore, "It's the truth. Kneeling on the floor in Will's room, I cried."

Braden had never seen his brother cry. Not once in all his life.

"Why?"

With a heavy sigh, he replied, "Because I'd finally run out of excuses and people to blame." Swallowing hard, Braden's chest felt heavy.

Admitting he was responsible for his life not turning out the way he wanted it to was all well and fine, but it wasn't going to do him any good. Liv was still gone.

"Charlotte didn't leave though."

Nodding, Auggie agreed, saying, "That's because she really wanted to stay." Drawing in a deep breath, Auggie appeared thoughtful.

"Ya know, Liv's not Charlotte."

"Nah, really?" Braden sarcastically replied before informing, "I blew it with her, man. From the beginning."

"Don't beat yourself up to bad. She was married when you met her," before taking the opportunity to poke fun at him saying, "Although that's never stopped you before." Braden laughed, before wrinkling his forehead in distress.

"I had her before Kieran. I just didn't know what I had."

"What?"

"Once in high school while Lily and I were broke up."

Auggie's eyes grew wide, "That was Liv?"

With a laugh, Braden assured, "I was surprised when I found out too," before admitting, "I don't even know what to do now."

"I don't either, but if you're gonna keep half-assing your way through life, then stop expecting things to turn out different than they always do." Braden nodded as the jailer walked up to the cell.

~

Charlotte was standing there waiting on them, when Auggie and Braden walked to the front of the police station.

"You know, somehow I always knew this day would come," she teased, curling the corner of her mouth into a smile.

Auggie wrapped his arm around Charlotte, kissing her on the cheek.

Braden smiled wide at her before asking, "Can we go?"

"Jackson and Emerson are still in there with the judge. All three of them are waiting to talk to you before you can go."

"Great," he complained before she informed, "Hey, be grateful. If it weren't for them your ass would be going to prison for assault." Braden nodded at her as she added, "And it didn't hurt that Ren had your back too."

"She did?"

"Mmhmm. She went and had a talk with Pat at the hospital. He won't be pressing charges."

Auggie laughed, "Lucky for him it was just a talk."

"Even her 'talks' scare me."

Charlotte laughed at Braden as she agreed with Auggie saying, "I think she may have invented the term badass."

6 months later...

Liv sat with her feet kicked up on a workbench in the shed behind her dad's house. It had become one of her favorite things to do since she arrived there. Watching Romeo create something beautiful out of something as simple as a piece of wood was nostalgic and serene. When she was growing up, Liv would spend hours watching him carve and design everything from cabinets to banisters. Now, she appreciated his keen eye for detail and the skillful craftsmanship that went into each of his creations.

Today was a good day to relax and watch him. It was taking her mind of what she needed to decide. It had been six month since she left town and she wasn't sure she could get out of going back.

"This Ren woman, she's important to you?" Blowing out a loud breath, Liv wasn't entirely prepared to explain everything to him. He had pretty much let everything lie, not pushing for answers, until now.

"Yeah."

Dusting off his hands, Romeo pulled a chair up next to hers questioning, "Why would you think twice about it then?"

Shrugging, she replied, "I'm not ready to go back."

"Because of 'man troubles'?"

Letting out a laugh, she shared, "Somethin' like that."

Slapping his hands against his knees, he stood up.

"You never struck me as the kind of girl that would run from a fight."

Crossing her arms across her chest, Liv assured, "I'm not."

"No?" Romeo argued. "Then what put you on a plane in the middle of the night and sent you here?"

"Nothing."

"I'm not a fan of you lyin'."

Swinging her feet off of the work bench, she planted them on the floor and stood up, griping, "No disrespect, but it's none of your business."

"Lillian Ingrid Vera," he stated in a gruff tone. "I haven't said a damn thing to you since you've been here. I let you have your space, but hell the only time you've left the house was to dye your hair purple."

Narrowing her eyes at him, she corrected, "Its grey with lavender highlights."

"I don't care if its traffic cone orange. You're hiding out here and I want to know why."

Shaking her head, she sat back down.

She thought time away was what she needed to get Braden out of her system and off of her mind, but neither happened.

"We're not good for each other."

Compassion shown in Romeo's eyes as he sat down next to her.

"I know I can be a hard ass sometimes but..." He started before she cut him off with a laugh assuring, "Not me and you."

A smile appeared on his face, then disappeared as he asked, "Says who?"

"I do."

"And who the hell are you?"

"What?"

"Don't what me. Does 'man troubles' feel the same?"

Closing her eyes for a moment, she remembered Braden telling her he was in love with her.

"No."

"So what makes you get to decide?"

Growing frustrated with him, she grumbled, "Aren't you supposed to be on my side?"

"Who says I'm not?"

Feeling put on the spot, Liv shared, "He lied to me."

"About?"

With a heavy sigh, she decided to tell him the whole story.

Leaving out the sex of course, her dad didn't need to know that. Liv filled him in on most of what had happened since the night Kieran died.

Scratching the side of his beard, he replied, "Sounds to me like he loves you."

"You should get your hearing checked."

"Maybe you need to take a listen to yourself."

"He lied."

"You ran."

Unable to stay seated, Liv hopped up, insisting, "I didn't run. He lied so I left." Seeing the expression on her dad's face was too much conviction for her to continue to look at him.

"If that's true, then what's the hitch with going back for an anniversary party?"

Forcing herself to reply, Liv stated, "There isn't one."

Romeo cocked a smile as he picked up his dremel.

Standing there, Liv watched as he walked back over to his woodworking. Her dad had argued her into going back. Damn him.

~

Lying in bed, Liv stared at her cell phone. She thought about texting Braden. It was the first time she had seriously considered it since she arrived at her dads. Wondering what he would say to her, if anything, she texted Penny.

L: I'm going.

Penny instantly texted back.

P: Yay! Are you going to stay at the farmhouse?

L: I don't know.

P: Do you want to stay with me and Seth?

L: I'll stay at the Inn if I don't.

P: I can't wait to see you! You should see me. I'm getting big.

L: Still no names?

P: Seth and I decided we would wait until he's born.

L: Why?

P: Well, what if we decide on Fred but he comes out looking like a John?

Liv laughed to herself. Only Penny would think like that.

L: Ha! See you soon.

P: :)

Smiling at Penny's smiley face, she missed her.

Liv missed everyone, especially Penny and Charlotte. Everything seemed to be going along fine without her there. Before she could help it, her thoughts switched back to Braden again. Was he going along fine without her too?

Her phone vibrated just as she was about to set it on the nightstand.

C: When are you coming? I can't deal with Sophia without you!

L: Ha! That bad?

C: I'm seriously about to knock her off her high horse.

L: I'll be there day after tomorrow.

C: Good! We'll have time to go shopping.

L: Try not to do any knocking off until I get back. I'd hate to miss it!

C: No promises. ;) By the way, Keylee is adorable. Still looks just like Ailin.

C: 'Night.

L: Later.

Setting her phone down, Liv closed her eyes. She wasn't entirely sure she would still consider it home, but she was going.

Braden's community service and probation were finally up and even though he planned on continuing to volunteer teaching a music class at the foundation Charlotte's father founded, it would now be voluntary. It was part of the agreement Jackson and Emerson had reached with the judge to keep him out of jail. A couple of years ago, he was there every week but somewhere in the mix of everything going wrong in his life, he stopped. It felt good to be back there, playing guitar and helping kids learn about music.

He had made peace with almost everything in his life. Selling the house he bought for he and Lily that she kicked him out of to marry Keven seemed to be a good starting point. He forgave Brooks and although it wasn't quite like it used to be, they became friends again. Instead of going back to work at Stockman's, which he was sure wasn't going to be a possibility, he used the money from the sale of his house to start his own business.

After taking his brother Auggie's advice to heart, concerning his tendency to half-ass most everything, Braden decided to finish Liv's library.

Whether she ever came back or not, it was important to him, that it be complete. As it turned out, finishing it was what had inspired him to go into business for himself. He wanted it to be perfect and when he couldn't find exactly what he wanted, Braden decided to make it himself. Countess instructional youtube videos and several calls to his cousin Oran concerning different types of wood and their durability aside, he had a knack for it.

Caffrey Customs seemed to fit what he did perfectly. From shelves to tables and chairs, all a customer had to do was give him an idea of what they wanted and he could build it. He enjoyed working for himself and creating unique pieces of furniture.

Content with the direction his life was now headed and happy for the most part, the only thing missing was Liv. Once again, he was the odd man out when he got together with his family but this time around, he didn't mind it as much. There was no substitute or replacement for her. He even had Penny tattoo her poem that he found on his left arm. Strange as it may seem, he wanted it there because she always sat to the left of him and somehow it made him feel like a part of her was still there next to him wherever he was.

It had been six months since Braden had seen or talked to her. He knew she was invited to Ren and Jacks' anniversary party, but no one said whether she was coming or not. While the majority of the time he longed to see her again, a small part of him wondered, if it was better not to, if she was just going to leave again. He missed her like crazy, she was what once made him whole. Things had changed since she left but he knew he would never truly be complete without her.

~

'Tear In My Heart' by Twenty One Pilots played from the speakers in Braden's workshop as he sanded the spindles of what was to be his nephews crib. It was late in the evening, but with all the orders that were coming in, he hadn't had time to work on it during the day like he'd planned. Penny was already seven months pregnant and he wanted to have it ready in time for her baby shower.

Braden looked up when the side door opened, smiling at his brother in law as he walked in.

"Penny got you out on another late night run?"

Seth laughed, "Yes, but I was happy to get out of the house."

"She driving you crazy?"

Shaking his head, Seth replied, "No, Sophia is and I know it's getting on her nerves too but she won't say anything."

"Yeah, it's always been like that between them. Is Ailin there too?"

"No, he's at your mom's with Keylee."

Braden stood up and placed the spindle he was sanding with the others.

"It's good that you escaped then," he laughed. "Wanna go grab a beer at The Dog House?"

"Sure, let me call Penny and see if she minds."

With a nod, Braden started picking up his work area.

Charlotte and Auggie were standing close to each other watching a table to the left of the bar when Braden and Seth arrived.

"What's going on?"

Charlotte smiled at Braden, explaining, "Brooks is trying to get Josephine to go home with him. He's been working on her for a good twenty minutes now."

Glaring in Brooks' direction, Seth said, "No way."

Auggie agreed, "That's what I said."

The four of them looked at each other.

When Liv left, Penny hired Josephine to help out around Legacy Ink. She seemed to get along well with Penny and Jimmy but aside from that, she mostly kept to herself. Her blonde hair was cut in a short bob that she often left a bit messy. No tattoos as far as anyone could see but she seemed to like piercings. Josephine definitely had a certain appeal. The kind that made you want to question who she was and where she came from. She was quiet with a serious expression constantly fixed on her face.

Braden pulled his wallet out of his back pocket, dug out a twenty and laid it on the bar.

"I have faith in my boy."

"She's just playing hard to get." Charlotte agreed before adding, "I'm in."

Auggie and Seth disagreed pulling out their wallets and placing their money on top of Braden's.

"Was that a smile?" Charlotte questioned as Braden answered, "Looks that way to me."

"Not the kind that says I'm going home with you." Auggie assured.

Seth added, "She's just being polite."

Seemingly out of nowhere, they watched as Josephine reached over and slapped Brooks right across his face.

In a triumphant tone, Auggie stated, "That's that then."

.."Umm, I don't think so." Charlotte said when Josephine then leaned over and kissed the cheek she had just slapped.

Pulling him close by the collar of his shirt, Josephine said something to him, then pushed him away and slapped him again.

"I don't know what's happening here." Seth shared as Josephine pulled Brooks back to her and into a long slow kiss.

Braden agreed, "I'm pretty lost too."
They were all stunned as Josephine stood up and slapped him a third time before coaxing him out of his chair and wrapping her arms around him as she grabbed his butt. When Brooks leaned in to kiss her, she let go and shoved him back, then quickly took his hand, kissed his cheek and lead him out of the door.

The four of them were quiet for a moment before Charlotte spoke up.

"I guess we can all just take our money back and maybe say a prayer for Brooks..."
Auggie cleared his throat before starting to laugh, while Seth and Braden where still reeling in confusion from what they had witnessed.

Having second thoughts about returning was an understatement. Even with her dad accompanying her, Liv felt like a nervous wreck. The flight was rough, which didn't help and neither did him getting the flight attendant's number before they landed.

After texting Charlotte and Penny to let them know she was back, Liv checked her dad and herself into the Better Valley Inn in town.

"You didn't have to get a room. You're welcome to stay at the farmhouse."

Romeo gave her a slight grin as he informed, "Might need the privacy."

Pausing for a moment, she gave him a questioning look.

"I'd be uncomfortable bringin' a woman home to your house."

With a slight smirk, Liv asked, "You mean there're women you didn't make it through the first time you were here?"

"One or two may have slipped through the cracks," he replied, raising an eyebrow at the curvaceous brunette behind the desk as she eyed him with an interested expression.

Shaking her head at Romeo, Liv took her key from the front desk clerk and headed to her room.

Knowing she needed to at least stop by the farmhouse to pick up her car, she sent Penny a text.

L: Can you take me to get my car?

P: I'm at Ren's with Sophia.

L: Okay.

P: Come to the bar tonight!

P: Everyone's going to be there.

Braden was part of the everyone. She thought she would have a little more time to work up to seeing him at the party.

L: The flight was rough, not really in the mood.

P: You don't have to stay. I'll be in the back with Charlotte. That way she can see you too.

L: Sounds like a plan, later.

Sitting down on the edge of the bed, it was a plan, but it didn't sound like a good plan at all.

Lying back against the bed, she wondered if he could still feel her thinking about him. Just the thought of seeing him was causing her stomach to clench up into rolling knots. Braden was the only man who had ever made her feel this way. Dying to feel alive. Eager to be subdued. Afraid of the fearlessness he invoked.

This needed to be over and there was only one way for that to happen. Sitting up, she blew out a loud breath. Shaking off whatever emotions were lingering, she had already done this once. She could do it again.

~

Parked in front of The Dog House, Liv stared at the doors. As she sat there psyching herself up to go in, Romeo interrupted her internal pep talk.

"We goin' in or do they come out and serve you at the curb here?"
Liv shot him an irritated glare as he cocked a smile at her.

"Your 'man troubles' must be in there."

Liv sucked in a hard breath before lying, "Nothing troubles me."

"Put your big girl pants on today, I see."

Rolling her eyes at her dad, she got out of their rental car.

The moment Liv stepped inside The Dog House, she was taken aback. Braden and Ailin were on stage singing 'Bartender Song' by Rehab while playing their guitars and Brooks was behind them on drums.

It was a confusing sight. One that made her heart joyful, and her thoughts cloudy as she made her way up to the bar. Auggie glanced in her direction then quickly scowled at her.

Clearly her change in hair color threw him off as he said, "Well, I'll be damned."

Still not over what was taking place on stage, she questioned, "Did I walk into some sort of a time warp?"

"Crazy huh," he replied before sharing, "Jacks gave the okay for a onetime thing."

Shaking her head she was still having a hard time understanding what was going on.

"This is my dad, Romeo," she introduced before turning and saying, "Dad, this is Auggie."

As they greeted each other with a handshake, Auggie uttered, "Ah hell, what can I get ya? On the house."

With an appreciative nod, Romeo replied, "Whiskey'd be nice."

"Charlotte and Penny in the back?" Liv asked as Auggie nodded and handed her dad his drink.

Nodding back, she headed towards the swinging doors that lead to Charlotte's office.

As soon as she opened the door to Charlotte's office, Penny jumped up and hugged her.

Hugging her back, Liv swore, "Gah, I missed you."

Charlotte stood up saying, "I love your hair," as she made her way over to them.

Penny stepped back, assuring, "It's so pretty."

Placing her hand on Penny's stomach, Liv said, "I didn't think you could get more beautiful, beautiful."

Reaching in to hug Liv, Charlotte agreed, "Isn't she gorgeous."

Liv nodded, hugging Charlotte before asking, "How do you feel?"

A cheery smile beamed on Penny's face as she replied, "Wonderful. I love being pregnant."
A sense of relief washed over Liv as she stood there with her friends.

Moving out of the doorway as Penny and Charlotte sat back down, Liv pulled up a chair.

"What the hell's goin' on out there?"

Charlotte laughed as Penny gave a soft smile saying, "It's been...interesting, since you left."

"We would have told you but you never asked."

"I'm askin' now." Liv blurted, curious to find out all that she had missed by being gone.

"Well, Braden got arrested." Charlotte started before Penny stopped her saying, "Brooks' car accident was first."

"What?"

Charlotte smiled saying, "Okay, we'll give you the shortest version possible."
Unable to get the thought of Braden being in jail out of her head, Liv nodded.

Penny and Charlotte took turns giving Liv the details on Brooks' accident, Braden kicking Pat's ass and getting arrested, along with Brooks and Auggie going to jail also. Lily's moving, Braden selling the house, and opening up Caffrey Customs.

"You weren't lyin' about interesting."
Charlotte and Penny stared at her as if they were wondering if she was going to ask any more questions.

When she just sat there, Charlotte asked, "So... You want to meet about one to go shopping tomorrow?"

Nodding Liv replied, "I'll meet you at your house."

Penny frowned slightly saying, "I guess you want me to take you to pick up your car now. I'm parked in the back"

Liv stood saying, "Yeah, let me go tell my dad I'm leaving."
She wanted to ask if Braden missed her, but she wasn't entirely sure she wanted to know at the moment.

Stepping out of the office, Liv closed the door behind herself, and then her eyes. It was a lot to take in.

Blowing out a breath, she opened her eyes and heard Braden say, "Liv."
His expression was perplexed, as if he wasn't sure that she was really there or not.

Heading for the swinging doors with a smirk, she snapped her fingers and pointed at him saying, "Hey, you recognized me this time."

~

Her words rolled through him causing the palms of his hands to ache. He couldn't help biting the side of his tongue as he smiled. She was really here.

Blocking her from moving forward, he took a step closer. "I'm diggin' the lavender."
She looked confused and he wasn't sure why, so he decided to keep talking.

"You down for Ren and Jacks' party?"

Her smirk was back, but only for a moment as she replied, "Can't say no to Ren."

She took a step back as he moved closer asking, "Are you staying at the farmhouse?"

"At the Inn. Penny's fixing to take me to get my car."
Braden was a bit relieved she hadn't been there. He wanted to be with her when she saw her library.

"I can take you."

Appearing as though she had to search for her words, Liv asked, "Are you playing at the party too?"

"They hired a DJ. Some nonsense about me having outbursts on stage."
Liv backed into the wall as she gave a nervous laugh without responding to his offer.

Braden could tell Liv was holding herself back. It was obvious she was fighting for control. Her body was calling to him, pleading to be touched. He could feel it.

"Let me take you," he offered as her lips parted and her shoulders pressed up against the wall.

"No."

"No?" he questioned taking a step back before saying, "Later."

Liv opened her mouth and then closed it. Stepping around him, she headed back into the bar.

Standing in the hallway, Braden stared at the swinging doors. Smiling to himself, he reveled in the feel of wanting her. Liv was back, and he had two days to do everything in his power to make her stay.

Braden felt wired and alive. As satisfying as his life had become, it was nothing compared to having her back, here and just inches from him.

He figured Liv left with her nowhere in sight when he walked back up to the bar.

Auggie was talking to an older man that he didn't recognize, when Braden interrupted their conversation to say, "Did you see her? You saw her. She's back."

"I know."

Invigorated, he assured, "She still wants me."

"Braden," Auggie replied, with a look of apprehension.

Ignoring his brother's look, he insisted, "It wasn't just sex for her either."

Auggie scowled shaking his head before motioning to the man he was talking to when Braden walked up.

"This is Romeo Vera, Liv's dad."

Braden felt his stomach drop as he looked at the man, who appeared to be about as old school hardcore as they come, sitting on the barstool next to him sipping a glass of whiskey.

Staring at Liv's dad, he had no idea what to do or say. There were definitely worse things he could have said in front of him, but there were also a hell of a lot better things too.

In an effort to turn the worst first impression he had ever made around, Braden held out his hand as he stated, "Mr. Vera."

Romeo turned his head in Braden's direction, raising an eyebrow as he looked him over.

His tone was gruff as he informed, "You're not what I expected."

"Sir?" Braden questioned, still holding his hand out even though it was clear her dad wasn't going to shake it.

"You drink?"

Lowering his hand, Braden replied, "Yes sir."

Nodding, Romeo suggested, "Sit down and have a drink then."

~

When Penny dropped Liv off at the farmhouse, she offered to stay with her for a while. After Liv declined, Penny headed home.

Liv sat on the porch. Her car started up right away, which was good. She knew they hadn't just let it sit for six months. She thought about going inside the house, then decided against it. Sitting there between an empty house and her car running in the driveway, she thought about Braden.

She was a liar. Liv had been so busy hiding behind his lie and what he had done wrong that she almost forgot about her own. She was in such a habit of lying to everyone around her she managed to start lying to herself along the way. The truth was, she never stopped having feelings for him from when she was a teenager. No matter how much she wanted to, she couldn't. Even falling in love with someone else didn't stop her from wanting him around. Although the feelings she held for Braden had changed many times over the years, they were always there.

Looking back on everything now, she took the opportunity to be honest with herself, about herself. She never would have cheated on Kieran physically, but then again where do you draw the line? If he had known she slept with Braden in high school, would Kieran have allowed him over? Would he have continued to let Braden be as big of a part of her life as he was at the time? Granted all things before Kieran were none of his business but this wasn't an estranged ex-boyfriend. It was his family. The answer was no. She never lied to Kieran it was more an omission of the truth. Liv wondered if Kieran was still alive and found out, would it hurt him to know she never told him? Would he be wounded to know that the man he so carelessly gave away her mark to, had once been the center of her world? She genuinely hoped so. That would make them even.

Standing up, Liv slowly stepped off of her porch and walked to her car. The possibility of starting over was there, it just wasn't possible here. Sliding into the driver's side of her car she scrolled through her playlist on her phone until 'Helena' by My Chemical Romance was blaring through her speakers.

On her way to the Inn, she knew there was no way to make any of this right. It was all built upon a lie anyway. Braden had come clean and was doing well without her there. Without her, he finally grew up and found his way. What had she done for the the last six months, aside from moping around her dads house? Nothing. It was possible at this point, she was even bad for herself. She would never be complete without him, but she loved him enough to keep up her front. The only truth that was important now wasn't that they were bad for each other, it was that she wasn't good for him.

It was a nice day of shopping with Charlotte. Liv didn't notice while she was staying at her dads, she was in desperate need for some girl time. Charlotte already had her dress for the anniversary party so the shopping part of their day didn't take long. It wasn't necessarily a formal occasion, more like dressy casual so when Liv found a pair of white wide leg trousers and a light grey silk v-neck ruffle wrap cami with spaghetti straps, she was satisfied with her selection. Not to mention the grey booties she picked up even though Charlotte frowned at her for choosing them over the strappy silver stiletto's she picked out.

All in all it was a relaxing day, until Charlotte decided to pry into her personal life on the way home.

"Are you going to hook up with Braden while you're down?"
Charlotte's question caught Liv so off guard that she had to slam on her brakes to keep from hitting the car in front of her.

"What?"

Curling the corner of her mouth into a smile, she asked, "What, as in you didn't hear me? Or you can't believe I asked you?"

With a laugh, Liv replied, "Oh, I believe you asked me."

"So..."

"Not a good idea."

"To ask you?"

"To sleep with him."

Charlotte was quiet for a minute or two before asking, "Are you seeing anyone?"

"No."

"Then why aren't you asking if Braden is seeing anyone?"

Ignoring her question, Liv continued to drive. Whether he was seeing someone or not wasn't going to change things.

"You're not going to answer me?"

Exhaling loudly, Liv griped, "Look, I know what you're doing. Don't."

"Whatever, Liv."

Glancing at Charlotte, she looked furious.

It was obvious she was mad. However, Liv didn't think she needed to explain herself to anyone.

"You're pissed off because I won't answer a question?"

Liv glanced over just in time to see the dirty look Charlotte was giving her.

"You didn't just leave Braden, ya know."

"What?"

Her voice was harsh as she fussed, "Don't what me. You know exactly what I'm saying to you. We're supposed to be friends and you didn't even say goodbye."

"Sorry." Liv snapped, irritated because Charlotte was making her feel bad.

"No you're not. What you are is blind. You don't see that you have friends here that care about you. No one cares if you get with Braden or not."

"They care so much that they hid the fact that Kieran was cheating?"

"Yes. As a matter of fact, that's exactly right. Augustus felt terrible when you left. And Seth doesn't have a mean bone in his body so why else would they?"

Shaking her head as she pulled up in Charlotte's driveway, Liv knew she was telling the truth. The night Liv found out, she was hurt and angry, but it didn't take long for her to move past it because she understood their motive.

Regardless, she didn't need Charlotte, who by the way, almost moved to another country when she and Auggie broke up, throwing it in her face.

"You must be spending too much time with Sophia lately, since suddenly you're all high and mighty."

Charlotte's eyes flew open wide and she looked as if Liv had slapped her. Grabbing her purse, she flung the passenger door open, jumped out and slammed the door.

Liv instantly opened her door and got out shouting, "Don't slam my door!"

Charlotte turned and made her way back to the car yelling, "You're lucky that's all I did!"
Shocked, Liv closed her door and walked to the front of her car.

"You wanna hit me?"

Tossing her purse on the ground, Charlotte hollered, "What if I do?"

~

Braden looked over at his brother and noticed he had stopped stirring his sauce.

"Do you hear that?"
Nodding, Auggie turned the burner off and headed towards his front door.

Following Auggie into the front yard, Braden could hear Liv and Charlotte before he saw them.

Neither were sure what to do as Charlotte pointed her finger in Liv's face shouting, "Do you want me to kick your ass," then Liv mocked, "Please, you can try."

"Are they fixing to fight?" Braden asked, looking at Auggie who shrugged shaking his head.

"And get your finger out of my face!" Liv snapped.
Charlotte moved her finger out from in front of Liv's face before poking her in the shoulder with

it. Liv narrowed her eyes at Charlotte, then poked her back.

It was hard at the moment to keep from laughing as he watched Liv and Charlotte take turns poking each other in the shoulder. When the poking accelerated into shoving, both Auggie and Braden stepped in.

Pulling Charlotte away from Liv, Auggie informed, "Alright, that's enough."
Liv started to take a step forward when Braden caught her and held her back.

Charlotte immediately snapped at Auggie, "Don't tell me what to do."
Pushing away from him, she gave the bottom of her shirt a little tug before turning back to Liv.

"You hurt my feelings."

Braden felt Liv relax in his arms as she replied, "I never meant to."

"I'm sorry I slammed your car door."

Liv gave her a soft smile, saying, "I'm sorry."
Charlotte smiled back at her and nodded before picking up her purse.

As Auggie and Charlotte stepped out of sight, it occurred to Braden that he was still holding onto her. She must have noticed at the same time because as soon as he looked at her, she started pulling away.

Adjusting his hands to get a better grip on her, he questioned, "Where are you going?"

In the time it took for her to stop moving and look at him, he was able to pull her all the way against him.

"Do you know how much I miss you?"

Her breathing picked up as she stared at him without answering.

"You miss me too."

Liv started to reply but he didn't give her the chance. Pressing his lips against hers, he wasn't letting her get away like he did last night.

There was no hesitation on her part. She instantly kissed him back. Holding onto him, she felt better than he remembered. He missed her. Time had somewhat dulled the ache he had for her, but now that she was back in his arms and he could taste her, a kiss was nowhere near enough.

Braden tried to slow their kiss but she was unrelenting. Liv was practically panting in between kisses and groping him in a way that was far from appropriate to be standing in his brother's front yard. He didn't want to stop, but at the same time, she wasn't giving him much of a choice unless he was planning on adding public lewdness to his criminal record.

"Liv..." he forced himself to say.

Freezing in place, it took a minute for her to move.

When she finally did, Liv appeared furious as she jerked away from him and blurted, "Shit!"
He tried to catch her but it was too late. She was out of his grasp and in her car before he could stop her.

Watching her car roll down the driveway before it burned off down the road, Braden leaned his back against the house. It would be easy to be mad at her for leaving him in the state he was now in because of her. However, the proof that she still wanted him was enough to outweigh the injustice. Smiling to himself, her body just gave away every lie she had ever told him.

Heading to the Inn, Liv needed a time to process what had just taken place. Hell, she needed several shots of the strongest liquor known to man and five years of intense meditation to make sense of it. The second Braden's lips touched hers, she couldn't catch her breath. She needed him. It was insane. It had only been six months. She remembered how wild and amazing it felt to be with him, and it didn't feel like that. All he did was kiss her.

When Liv arrived back at the Inn, her dad was stepping out of his room as she was going into hers.

"You're back."

Avoiding eye contact with him, she quickly uttered, "Not now dad," and closed herself in the room.

"Do you remember Joe from Almer Street?" he questioned through the door.

After thinking for a minute, she replied, "Yeah."

"I'm meeting him for dinner."

"Okay."

"Want me to bring you back somethin'?"

"No thanks."

Liv waited to see if her dad was going to say anything else before she walked away from the door and sat down on the bed.

She needed to think clearly but it was impossible. Feeling as if she was being pulled apart, her head, body and heart were all moving in three completely different directions. The only real problem with her indecision was the one thing they all had in common. Braden.

Pulling out her cellphone, Liv leaned back against the bed.

L: I can't...
B: Can't what?
L: I need to say goodbye.
B: I know.
L: Can you come over?"
B: Where are you?
L: Room 39.

Dropping her phone next to her on the bed, she thought maybe all she needed was to get him out of her system.

It seemed like a good idea, possibly one that would benefit them both. Of course there would be sex, but in the mix, one final goodbye. Unlike before, there was no chance of her being caught off guard or swept off of her feet by the moment. Even when she saw her words permanently marked on his skin, there weren't enough love poems to undo what had already been done. Time was an issue, however, they had until tomorrow afternoon to be out of each other's systems. She would do things right this time. Attend Ren and Jack's anniversary party, tell her friends goodbye and leave town the next morning. Then she and Braden could go on with their own separate lives.

The knock on her door startled her, even though she knew it was coming. Liv's body seemed to vibrate with anticipation as she slowly made her way over to open it.

When she let Braden into her room, he walked past her and sat down on a chair in the corner instead of on the bed.

As Liv sat on the edge of the bed and faced him, Braden shared, "I'm not who I was when you left."

Silently, she nodded at him.

"And I'm still not the man I should be."

Liv's breathing grew shallow as she hung on his every word.

"I'm not as empty as I once was, but I doubt I'll ever be completely whole."

She started to speak then stopped as he held up his hand.

"There's always going to be something missing inside of me without you," he swore before he stood up. "But if you don't feel the same, then let's finish this."

There was a moment of hesitation as Liv agreed. It was the last lie she would tell him, but she couldn't bring herself to say it out loud.

Standing up, she tilted her head down as she closed her eyes. Everything fell away with the sensation of his touch. He was right. Neither one of them would ever be compete without the other, but there was no need to let the void control their lives. There was no meant to be, no fate to control what happened next, the destiny that lay ahead of them was a choice, and she made it for both of them.

Saying goodbye to Liv was the hardest moment of Braden life. Harder than seeing her broken and suffering, even harder than the anguish he felt finding out she left. If it weren't for knowing their goodbye was the only way to truly end things in order for them both to have a new beginning, leaving her while she slept in the middle of the night may have done him in completely.

~

Waking up alone after falling asleep in Braden's arms hurt Liv's heart. However, since the pain was self-inflicted, it was enough to secure her guard back in place where it belonged. She could now leave without sorrow. There was no loss here. Only surrender to what was good for both of them. That kind of pain, she could deal with.

~

The night was lit by a mixture of stars in the summer sky and tiny white lights hanging from the trees. Music played loudly from the DJ booth set up on Ren and Jacks' back porch, making it a pleasant volume as it filtered out into the yard among the guests and their conversations.

Family and friends roamed the property, visiting with each other and congratulating the couple that was legendary in their family for proving real love could endure everything. Braden stood with his brother Ailin waiting for their mom Sarah to show up.

"Do you miss it?"

Ailin shook his head questioning, "Miss what?"

With a shrug Braden replied, "The way things used to be."

"I miss y'all and Will of course. It's kinda strange though, knowing Keylee won't grow up here."

Braden smiled teasing, "Don't worry, we can still corrupt her from a distance."

Laughing, Ailin agreed, "And how the hell is Auggie her favorite? I'm going to have to lock her up when she's a teenager if that's a hint of what's to come."

"Nah, she's one of us. It's the other kids parents that'll need to worry."

As they laughed together, Penny and Seth walked up.

"Mom's still not here?" she questioned, appearing a bit put out.

Seth stated, "I'm sure she's on her way."

Whipping her head around, she snapped at him. "How do you know?"

"I don't. I'm sorry. I love you."

Shaking her head she started to cry, "Why am I so hot?"

Braden stared at his sister, trying to figure out why that was worth crying over.

"Would you like me to get you some ice?" Seth offer, in a compassionately smooth tone.

Just as quickly as Penny started crying, she stopped.

Pushing up on the toes of her sandals, she gave him a cheery smile saying, "I love you." Wrapping her arms around his neck she pulled him close for a short kiss before informing, "I'll just go get some."

As she walked away, Braden couldn't help blurting, "That was frightening."

"You have no idea." Seth assured before Ailin sympathized by patting Seth on the shoulder, saying, "I remember those days."

Seth instantly looked up as Penny shouted, "Are you coming or what?"

"Yes, baby, I love you," he answered, taking off after her.

Shaking his head, Braden started laughing again.

Not long after Penny and Seth stepped away, Auggie and Charlotte showed up.

"Lookin' pretty sharp there, brother." Braden said, complimenting Auggie's tan suit that matched nicely to his wife's dress.

Holding his hand, Charlotte leaned into Auggie from the side as she blurted, "Doesn't he look sexy."

"No," both Braden and Ailin replied before another voice came from behind saying, "I kinda think he does."

Charlotte laughed, noting, "See," as Liv nudged Auggie with her shoulder and winked at him.

Romeo was right beside her assuring, "That's fine for boys. Men are debonair."
Braden, Ailin, and Auggie gave Romeo a nod as another voice interrupted them.

Braden was slightly shocked to see his mom. Not because she was finally there but because of the way she looked. Her auburn hair that was normally pinned up in a bun or kept back in a long braid was down, making her look younger. And she was wearing makeup.

"Where is your sister?" Sarah griped at them.

Braden thought, at least she sounded the same as he replied, "She had a mini melt down and went to get some ice."

"Wow, Sarah, you look nice." Charlotte complemented, earning her a sarcastic smile before Liv asked, "What's got you all dolled up?"

"I'm so glad you're back." Sarah mocked as she eyed, Romeo. "Isn't he a little old for you?"

Romeo cocked an eyebrow at Sarah as he answered, "I would hope so, I'm her dad."

Sarah's let a light smile slip as she replied, "Oh." Holding out her hand to him, introducing herself. "Sarah."

Taking it, he kissed the top of her hand and stated, "Romeo."

The smile spread across her face as she offered, "Would you like to get a drink?"
Romeo nodded at her before they walked off together.

Everyone stood there in a sort of stunned silence for a moment.

"What the hell was that?" Auggie griped, saying what everyone else was thinking.

Liv smirked saying, "My dad's always had a thing for red heads."

Auggie scowled at her fussing, "What the..." before Charlotte cut him off, patting his arm.

"Now, Augustus, I'm sure Sarah knows what she's doing." Then with a wicked smile as if she couldn't resist, she added, "And later she'll be hookin' up with Liv's dad."

"Ha!" Liv blurted as Auggie drug Charlotte away saying, "Come on were going to go get a drink."

Ailin shook his head saying, "Yeah, I better go see if Sophia ever got Keylee to sleep." Before he walked off towards the house.
Then it was just the two of them.

When Liv glanced at him, Braden could feel the tear in his heart. She was leaving in the morning.

"Ya know what I find odd?"

Wrinkling up his forehead, he turned to face her.

"They're celebrating ten years, when they spent a lifetime loving each other."

Braden thought for a moment before sharing, "Maybe it's easier to love someone than to really be with them."

"You may be right."

Flashing a smile at her, he turned and walked towards the party.

~

The evening wound down as it got to be close to midnight and guests started to leave. The pain Braden was experiencing knowing what was to come started to weigh on him as he felt an arm slide around his waist. Looking down, he saw a pair of beautiful grey eyes staring up at him.

"Did you have a nice time tonight?"

Smiling at Ren, he nodded.

"Do you remember when we met?" she asked, letting go of him as she tucked a few strands of her long brown hair behind her ear.

With a laugh, he replied, "Yeah, me and Auggie gave you hell 'cause I asked you if you were gonna kiss Jacks."

Rolling her eyes she gave him a sincere smile. "We wasted a lot of time, waiting for the right time."

Braden found it hard to smile, thinking of what love really does to people.

"Braden." Ren stated before glancing at Liv and then back up at him. "Stop wasting time."
Ren reached down and squeezed his hand. When she let go, she turned and walked back to her husband Jacks.

Braden watched Ren slide her arms around her husband as he leaned down and kissed her. Their love story was epic, but she was right. What was the point of fighting the good fight for years when he could throw down right now?

Hugging Penny and Charlotte as she was getting ready to leave, Liv promised to stop by and see them on her way out tomorrow. It was going to be a long drive with her dad to get back to his house and just the thought of driving for thirty six hours was already making her tired.

She was about to interrupt whatever conversation Romeo and Sarah had been holding all night, so they could go back to the hotel, when Braden stopped her.

"You still owe me a dance."

"What?"

Smiling at her, he reminded, "Remember, at Auggie and Charlotte's wedding? You were going to dance with me, then you said you would catch me next go round."

She did remember.

"They're not playing music anymore."

As soon as the words left her mouth, 'Hallelujah' by Rufus Wainwright started to play.

Liv gave him a suspicious glare, but didn't fight it when he led her a few feet away from her dad and his mom. The song was rather appropriate after all that had been said and done between them.

Braden held her in his arms. As they swayed back and forth to the music, Braden hummed along with the song until it was almost to the end.

Whispering in her ear, "Remember when I moved in you... Every breath we drew was hallelujah..."

She was so moved by Braden holding her, the song, and his whisper, she slid her hands to the sides of his face, allowing him to rest his forehead against hers.

"Let's get married," he murmured, like it was nothing.

Quickly letting go of him, she blurted, "What?"

"I love you."

Shaking her head at him, Liv couldn't believe he was doing this to her.

It was too late for him to say those things. Yesterday when he said his piece, he agreed. It was over. Twice now, Braden had told her that he loved her and both times, it was almost like a last resort. Now he was throwing marriage at her to try and keep her there. Who wants to be someone's afterthought? Liv's mind spun in a thousand different directions, reliving moments with him as well as imagining different scenarios. He couldn't do that to her. Tell her things. The things that should have already been said, just because he wanted to keep her around.

Pushing against him, she barked, "You're an asshole."

Walking away from him as fast as she could, she heard Braden call after her.

Her dad shouted, "Lillian!" But she didn't care.

Sprinting to her car, she stopped when she reached it. Frantically pulling at the handle she needed it to open, but her dad had the keys.

Finally she heard a pop as the door unlocked.

"Other side. You're not driving."

Thankful she was getting out of there and away from Braden, she didn't argue with Romeo.

~

Still standing in the exact spot where he danced with Liv, Braden stared at his sister.

"Why did he call her that?"

Charlotte answered for her, saying, "Because that's her name."

Confused, he argued, "Liv's not short for Lillian."

"No, her middle name is Ingrid. Liv is her initials. Or they were before she was Caffrey." Penny shared.

How could he have known her for so long and not known that?

He recalled, Lily's 'good luck with your new Lilly'. She must have remembered her from high school, even though he didn't. What were the chances that he ended up on the losing end of another Lily? He had to wonder if that was why things didn't seem to work out no matter how hard he tried. Maybe the name was cursed. Like him. His tattoo instantly came to mind. Liv practically freaked out when he was going to take his shirt off after bringing her storage bins into the house. Then when she actually saw it, at Brennen's cabin, she couldn't take her eyes off of it. The night Kieran gave it to him, he said 'You're taking the mark of someone's heart that doesn't belong to you'. At the time, Braden just thought that Kieran was pissed and being an ass because he wouldn't take no for an answer.

Heat started to spread throughout his entire body as he looked at his mom.

"Did you give me Liv's mark?"

Pursing her lips at him, Sarah scoffed, "I gave you one that she drew."

"How did that happen?"

Auggie scowled at him as he explained, "When Kieran went to mom with the Lily, he had her draw him a different one."

Shaking his head, he couldn't believe that no one told him.

"Why didn't Liv stop him?"

Charlotte cleared her throat, saying, "She didn't find out until a few months after you got it."

"Honestly, son, it's not that big of a deal."

Giving her mom a dirty look, Penny took a few steps forward informing, "Yes it is. Whether you believe in it or not, you gave Liv your heart when you took her mark."

Glaring at Penny, Sarah argued, "Getting a tattoo doesn't make you fall in love with someone."

Ignoring her mom, Penny stressed, "Think about it, Braden. Do you really think it's a coincidence?"

~

They reached the hotel after an agonizingly quiet drive. Liv knew there was no way Romeo was going to let what happened at the party go. It wasn't in his nature to not question her.

Romeo turned the car off, holding the keys in his hand as he demanded, "Answers. Now, Lillian."

"I'm a grown woman."

His tone was harsh as he assured, "When you start acting like one, I'll treat you like one."

"I can't believe you're on his side."

Romeo's eyes softened as he replied, "I'm not on his side."

"Then why aren't you questioning him?"

"Is he in this car? Is he my daughter?"

Rolling her eyes, Liv made an irritated noise and looked away.

The car was silent for a moment before he shared, "You can't be mad at him for loving you."

"Who says I am?"

"I do."

Leaning her head back against the headrest, Liv blew out a loud breath saying, "It's all just one big lie."

"Not to him. That boy's in love with you."

Shaking her head, Liv argued, "We're wrong for each other. He knows it too. He said it himself that he's not the man he needs to be. That's because of me. Something happens when we're together. We can't move past each other. It's not right."

"Look at me Lillian," he stated as she turned her head in his direction. "Now, you listen to your old man."

Feeling desperate, she nodded.

"Men are strange creatures, constantly at war with themselves on the inside. We're designed to sabotage ourselves. It's the woman though... The one that gives him something to fight for that makes him the man he needs to be. There's no good, bad, right or wrong to it. It's the victory he's after. You're either the prize or a casualty. And that my girl, is the only decision that's up to you."

Romeo patted her on the arm before opening the driver's side door. Dropping her keys in the seat as he got out, he closed the door, and walked into the Inn.

Braden shook his head as he pulled up to the farmhouse. It just figured that they would end up in the same place. Maybe this was fate.

Walking into the house, he wouldn't have to look for her this time. Braden knew exactly where he would find her. Stepping into her library, she was standing in the center of the room, staring at her bookshelf.

"Liv."

Slowly turning around she stated, "No."

"I didn't ask you anything."

Shaking her head at him she replied, "It doesn't matter. The answer is always going to be no."

With a slight laugh he informed, "Good to know all my hard work was for nothing."

Narrowing her eyes at him she questioned, "What?"

"I was going to ask how you liked your library."

Blowing out a loud breath she turned her back on him.

"Why did you do this?"

"I wanted to finish what I started."

"I left."

"It wasn't about you anymore. I finished it for me."

Nodding, she remained silent this time.

The longer Liv stood there quietly. The angrier he grew at her. How could she? All this time, he thought something was wrong with him, and it turned out it was her. It was always her.

"I'm gonna need you to turn around and look at me."

As if she knew what was coming, Liv hesitantly turned and faced him.

"Kieran never really loved you."

Instantly her eyes showed all the hurt that Braden intentionally inflicted.

"Oh, I'm sorry. That was an asshole thing to say, wasn't it?"

Her eyes narrowed at him, in response.

"The truth hurts doesn't it, Liv."

"You would know," she spouted, with a nasty smirk across her face.

"Did you ever let him see the real you? The one I got glimpses of here?"

Liv's smirk disappeared as she shook her head.

Without knowing if she was answering him or simply shaking her head at what he was saying, he continued, "He couldn't have loved the real you. The one I had the privilege of seeing at the cabin."

He stepped closer to her.

Liv shuddered as Braden ran his finger down the guitar tattoo on the inside of her arm.

"I know he didn't, because if he did, I wouldn't have your mark and you wouldn't have mine."

Her eyes softened under his touch.

Tracing the B and then the C that made up the body of the guitar, he shared, "I bet he never even noticed did he."

Braden could see her struggling as she swallowing hard, trying to pretend.

"That doesn't matter. What matters is..."

Tired of the dishonesty surrounding them, he cut her off.

"You can lie to me as much as you want, but stop lying to yourself. Kieran loved the idea of you, not you. That's why it didn't last. Just like Lily and me."

Liv jerked her arm away, fussing, "Don't compare me to her."

"I wasn't, I was comparing myself to Kieran."

Appearing stunned, she took a step back.

Compassion filled her eyes as Liv glanced around her library.

"You're not like he was."

Nodding, Braden replied, "With you I'm not. With her I was."

Pausing he took a deep breath and closed the distance between them.

"And you're so in love with me I can feel it coming off of you. Just admit you feel guilty because you never stopped loving me. I was your first everything. That's why my initials are on you and there's not a single K on your body. You're always going to be in love with me. Just like I'm never going to stop being in love with you."

Tears welled in Liv's eyes as she stared at him.

Placing his hands on the sides of her face, this was it. It was the make or break moment of Braden's life.

"It could be fate."

His hands fell from her face as she took a step back.

"There's no such thing."

"We're meant to be together."

Liv closed her eyes causing a tear to escape and roll down her cheek.

"It's only ink."

The banging on Liv's door at the Inn was making it hard for her to focus as she dug through her suitcase.

"Open the door!" Auggie's voice boomed from the other side.

What the hell was his problem?

Giving up on getting dressed, she grabbed a robe from behind the bathroom door, shouting back, "Hang on!"

Wrapping the robe around herself, Liv pushed the door of a narrow coat closet shut and opened the door to let him in.

Auggie was already scowling at her as he walked in.

Without the most pleasant attitude toward him, she griped, "What's up?"

Glaring at her open suitcase, he snapped, "You're really gonna leave him? Again?"

"Is that your business?"

"Damn right, he's my brother."

"And?" she questioned.

"He's in love with you." Auggie fussed at her.

Irritated, she griped, "What's that got to do with you?"

"I don't want to see him get hurt again."

Shaking her head at him, Liv spouted, "I see. You want me to stay so you don't feel like you failed as a big brother."

His face grew solemn as he replied, "I'm tryin' to help. The both of you."

"Ha!" she blurted before sharing, "I think you've 'helped' enough, already."

Liv could see how frustrated he was getting with her as he ran his hand down the front of his beard.

"Look, Auggs, I know you're tryin' to look out for him, but what went down between Braden and me last night had nothing to do with you. You have no say so in what happens next."

Liv walked back to the door and opened it.

She knew Auggie loved his brother and was sincerely trying to help, but Braden was a grown man and the sooner Auggie started treating him like one, instead of like a lost little boy, the better off their relationship would be.

"I have a lot to do before I leave here, so thanks for stopping by." Liv stated with a smirk on her face.

Auggie started to walk out, then stopped to look at her as he said, "Maybe you should get your head out of your ass and give him a real shot, not for me or him, but because you're in love with him."

Liv narrowed her eyes at him, swinging the door closed behind him as he walked out.

Mumbling to herself, she sat down on the end of the bed. Auggie needed to learn how to mind his own business, but he was right. She was in love with him, and last night after she shot down his idea that they were destined to be together, Braden got down on one knee.

Holding an entwined circle of guitar string, he informed, "All these years I kept my first set of strings. I never thought much about why, until you left." Holding onto her hand, Braden shared, "I wasn't destined to play guitar. It wasn't fate that I picked it up. I made it happen, because I wanted it." Sliding the guitar string ring onto her ring finger he informed, "All it takes is for you to want it too."

She sat there for a minute, glancing around the room.

"He's gone."

Liv smiled wide as Braden opened the coat closet and stepped out saying, "Well, that was frickin' awkward."

Eying his naked body as he made his way over too her, she looked at the lily on his chest then her poem on his arm.

Pushing her back onto the bed, he asked, "Where were we?"

"Since I had already successfully pulled my head from my ass, you were saying something about loving me."

Biting the side of his tongue as he smiled wide at her, Braden replied, "Oh, yeah." As he untied her robe and slid his hands inside of it.

Leaning in, he gave her a long slow kiss.

In seconds, Braden had her out of her robe and underneath him.

Pushing into her as her legs wrapped around his waist, Braden swore, "I'm gonna love you like no man has ever loved a woman before."

Liv's breathing grew heavy as she replied, "Is that all?"

As he picked up his pace he added, "I'm also gonna to think of new ways to put it to you, every day."

She let out a, "Ha," before he closed her mouth with his kiss.

Her hands slid into his hair, tugging on it as she fiercely kissed him back.

Pulling back, just in time to hear his name fall from her lips, Braden kissed her again, until neither one could hold out any longer.

In awe of her peaceful breathing as she leaned her head back and closed her eyes, Braden asked, "So, Fairmont's on the Lake?"

She smiled.

"Yes."

Rolling them both over, he wrapped his leg around hers holding her close to his body.

"Another yes?"

Nibbling on the edge of his jaw, she stated, "It will always be yes."

The End

Marked Heart Series
Epilogue

Turning the knob to open the door, Ren sighed as Jacks moved her hand away.

"We're going to be late."

Flashing a wide smile at her, he slid his hands into the back of her hair, coaxing, "Just one more."

Ren leaned her head back and closed her eyes, only to receive a quick peck on her lips.

"That was...weak," she laughed, expecting much more from his kiss.

Another wide smile preceded his saying, "You, my beautiful wife, said we were going to be late."

"Fine." Ren pretended to pout before asking, "Are you going to offer Seth the position today?"

"I think I'll wait 'til Monday, bringing home a baby and being asked to take over JPT Financial may be a little much for him all in one day."

Arching an eyebrow at her husband, she questioned, "If he says yes, and you retire early, what are you going to do with all that free time, Mr. Thomas?"

"We," he clarified, wrapping his arms around her tight, "Will be having lots of sex, Mrs. Thomas. And maybe travel a little."

Shaking her head at him with a laugh, she said, "Alright, Jacks. Let's go before we really are late."

As Ren started to open the door again, Jackson stopped her. Wrapping his arms around her, he leaned her back, kissing her without restraint.

~

Crossing her arms across her chest, Charlotte gave Auggie a dirty look as he drove.

"You do know you're insane, right?"

Glancing over at her with a scowl on his face, Auggie replied, "What? I think it's reasonable."

"Augustus, you cannot suggest they give him Caffrey as a last name."

Appearing offended, he griped, "Why not?"

"Are you serious?"

"What kinda name is Chevalier anyway?"

"Its French and I think it means Knight."

Auggie took the opportunity to glare at her when he stopped at a red light.

"No tellin' what they're naming him with a frilly last name like that."

With a slight huff, she reminded, "That's why we are going over there."

"And that's another thing..." he started before Charlotte cut him off saying, "Oh-kay."

Scowling at her as he continued driving, Auggie fussed, "What if one day I wanna hand the bar over to him, like Jacks just did to us?"

Curling the corner of her mouth into a smile, Charlotte teased, "Then it'll be an 'Ah hell, there's a Frenchman runnin' The Dog House' moment."

"I think that may have cut my soul a little..."

With a sly smile, Charlotte offered, "Awe, if you pull over I'll kiss it and make it better. That is, unless you're scared."

~

Seth loaded Penny's suitcase into the trunk before walking to the side of his car. Leaning in through the open back door, he gently kissed Penny.

"Are you sure you don't need anything?"

Penny gave a cheerful smile as she assured, "We're fine. I'm sure everyone's at the house waiting on us."

Nodding, he carefully placed his hand on his son, saying, "I don't mind sharing the number one spot with this little guy in your top ten."

"It's really our top ten. Every great moment, they've all been with you."

Seth kissed her again, saying, "He's the first. Before you know it we're going to have a house full of number one's."

Penny giggled, checking the car seat one last time, to make sure her son was strapped in tight, as she suggested, "We should get this one home, so he can meet his family."

~

Parked against the curb in front of Penny and Seth's house, while 'Could Have Been Me' by Struts played over the radio, Braden sat leaned up against the inside of his car door. With one leg kicked up onto the bench seat of his El Camino, Liv sat between his legs, her back against his chest. His arms rested comfortably around her as he held her hands in her lap, rubbing his thumb against her guitar string engagement ring that she kept as her wedding band.

Placing light kisses against her temple, he asked, "You feelin' better?"

Nodding, she brought his left hand to her lips.

Kissing the Liv tattoo Braden had Penny give him, in lieu of a wedding band on his ring finger, she replied, "Now that we're stopped."

Braden slid his hand to her stomach, right below her belly button, saying, "Ya know, in a little over six months we'll be bringing our own lil' Liv or Braden home."

Tilting her chin up, she turned her head toward his and kissed him.

"While we're waiting..." Braden whispered against her mouth as his fingers inched a bit lower.

Just as Braden deepened their kiss, they heard another car pull up.

"Hold that thought." Liv said with a slight laugh.

~

Sarah and Romeo arrived, prompting Braden and Liv to get out of the car. Charlotte and Auggie pulled up right after and then Ren and Jacks.

Everyone greeted one another as they stood on the porch waiting for Penny and Seth to show up and properly introduce the newest addition to their family.

"Are you down for good now?" Jackson asked Romeo.

Wrapping his arm around Sarah's waist, he replied, "I have one more trip back then she's stuck with me for good."

Just as Auggie was about to say something about his mom and Liv's dad moving in together, Penny and Seth showed up.

They crowded around Penny and the baby as Seth unlocked the door. Once everyone was settled in the house, Seth set up his laptop so that Sophia and Ailin were able to join in over video chat.

Seth lifted his son out of his car seat and handed him to Penny. The room was silent as they anxiously awaited hearing the name of the sleeping baby boy with dark blue eyes and a head full of reddish brown hair.

Snuggling her son in her arms, Penny revealed, "We decided on, William Augustus Chevalier."

The room remained quiet until they heard Sophia and Ailin's daughter, Keylee, over the laptop ask, "Mommy, why are you crying?"

Penny's cheery smile started to fade as she noticed most everyone in the room had a solemn expression or tears in their eyes.

"Y'all don't like it?" she questioned before the room erupted in smiles and laughter.

Everyone assured Penny, she and Seth couldn't have picked a better name before taking turns holding and instantly falling in love with William.

~

No matter what losses are suffered in life, for there will always be pain, never lose sight of love. There is strength in the ability to accept and to give love. It takes you past your scars, beyond your fears, and forever lays a permanent mark upon your heart. Love endures everything.

Playlist

Music has a way of inspiring the smallest ideas. It allows me to create an entire scene or chapter from just the right song. For me, music is one of the most important creative tools there is. These are the songs that brought Marked Heart to life.

21 Guns
GreenDay

The Man Who Broke His Own Heart
Everclear

Believe
Mumford & Sons

Back To The Shack
Weezer

Come And Get Your Love
Redbone

Halleluja
Rufus Wainwright

Tear In My Heart
Twenty One Pilots

Hollow Moon(Bad Wolf)
AWOLNATION

Scars
Papa Roach

The Judge
Twenty One Pilots

Bartender Song
Rehab

Helena
My Chemical Romance

Could Have Been Me
The Struts

Marked Heart Series

Enduring Everything
MH#1
Available Now

Time doesn't always heal old wounds. Often time makes them worse. Especially when you push those wounds to the back of your mind and focus on the life you want to lead. Then the day comes when you finally have everything. It is then, you realize that nothing ever goes away.

Charlotte
MH#2
Available Now

The true measure of a person's worth lies not within what they can offer you but what you have to offer them. No matter how desirable, are they worth your time, patience, forgiveness, loyalty, friendship, love, respect, understanding, compassion, trust? If not, they are worth more than you have to offer. They deserve for you to let them go.

One Penny
MH#3
Available Now

Foolish is the heart that leaves itself open to falling in love. Reckless is the person who steps away from tradition to claim a life of their own. Irreplaceable is the moment one takes the risk.

C&A Novella
MH#3.5
Available Now

He was all the things she really wanted and never bothered to look for in a man. He was also the most stubborn jackass she had ever met.

She was an infuriating pain in the ass, and he'd be damned straight to hell if he had to spend even one day without her by his side.

Marked Heart
MH#4
New Release

A marked heart, longing for the one is nothing more than a restless heart, burdened by a lie.

Acknowledgments

It's not easy being Mr. M. but hubs pulls it off. Or takes it like a champ. Either way, he hasn't left me yet, so, that's a win. It's because of him that I know what real love is.

And the kids? Yeah, they're pretty awesome too!

Thank you to my readers! Without y'all my characters would never see the light of day.

All the Indie blogger/reviewer/supporters out there, I appreciate everything that you do to keep us writers writing.

Susanne Lancello, Nicole Griffin, Lucii Grubb, Sonya Ray, Katelynn Luna, Paula Genereau, Carmen Paez y'all rock harder than Liv's sexy socks ♥.

To my Street Team, I appreciate everything you ladies do!

About the Author

M. Sembera was born in Baton Rouge, Louisiana and now lives in Brazoria, Texas with her husband, three kids, three dogs and two cats. After writing her first short story when she was in high school, M. instantly fell in love with writing. However, life sometimes gets in the way of aspirations and it wasn't until years later, when her life calmed down, M. was able to start writing again.

'For me, each new book I write or character I create feels like the first time and I find myself falling in love with writing all over again'

Receive updates and info on author M. Sembera's New Releases, WIPs, Sales and Giveaways by subscribing to M's monthly newsletter: http://eepurl.com/bdJ_Uj

Work in Progress

Be on the look out for the re-release of the series that started it all:

The Rennillia Series

Set in a small southern town, death, love, hurt, friendship and anger bond Rennillia Cantinelli, Scott Herterand, Emerson Roberts and Jackson Thomas while shaping the paths they will follow into adulthood.

After a six year separation from her friends, Ren returns to the Roberts' house to start over.

Caught between love, loyalty, friendship and restrained by obligations, these four discover the bond they formed long ago is not the only thing holding them together.

Rennillia 1- November 2015

Rennillia 2- January 2016

Rennillia Prequel- March 2016

Rennillia 3- May 2016

www.ingramcontent.com/pod-product-compliance
Lightning Source LLC
Chambersburg PA
CBHW051411170626
46809CB00006B/2111